THE LAST ORTOR

G. ROCHELLE

ACKNOWLEDGMENTS

To my family and best friend: You all always told me I could do it! Thank you for encouraging me to continue writing.

To my strongest supporter, my husband: You are my rock! Thank you for always believing in me and my will to write. Thank you for pushing me in all the right places to complete this work.

I give thanks to The One Above, who imbues everyone with beautiful talents and strengths. To Him, credit is due for helping me every step of the way, and gifting me with the love of art and creation through words and stories.

To my patient editors: It was a journey, thank you for making it go smoothly.

Do Not Read It.
This Book Is Not for You.

~ Magic ... Love ... Secrets ~

ANGELA

Spring
Early 1970s

My dearest daughter, if you are reading this, you are unharmed. I procured the safe in which this letter rests, hoping to someday pass its contents onto my children. I only had a single daughter, and so that means that everything herein is yours. It belongs solely to you.

— A LETTER

Angela was not the type of girl to be late, but she had overslept today, still unusual for her. It was because of the Roe case. It was different. Maybe the biggest in history. It's not the type of thing everyone can put away at a convenient night-time hour. This necessitated the loss of sleep. She was sure the studio would forgive her; she'd broken more cold cases than anyone there. She was well known, and well-loved. She picked up the documents from the coffee table, hugging them against her chest. These documents were everything. Months of research. She didn't have time to place them into her bag and ignored the ringing phone. It was probably Ed calling to check up on her. She stumbled a bit as she wrapped a light scarf around her neck. Thankfully, the rain stopped, but it left cold puddles that evaded Angel's attention.

She had to cover for John, and she hated covering for him. She was due to be on air in exactly ten minutes. It could take up to twenty to get to the studio. She rushed down the street, worried about being even more late than originally expected. Catching a cab would not be wise in this traffic. She looked around Madison Avenue as though within its limits it held some clue—the key to a prompt arrival.

If she didn't miss the train, the ride would take about thirteen minutes. Then a two or three-minute walk to the studio. She kept on telling herself, that the crew would be fine with it. They adored her anyway.

She ran across the street toward the train station. Traffic was super slow; the cabs were moving at a turtle's pace. She made a run for it. Something heavy collided with her, hitting just below her rib cage. She lost feeling and control in her limbs, sending her precious work flying. She watched as the wafted papers descended, meeting the pavement nearby just as she felt the impact of meeting the ground. Her head spiraled, and her vision blurred in a foggy haze. She heard the fearful screams of unfortunate witnesses before the darkness overtook her.

❧

Somewhere in the distance, through the fog, she heard voices again. As the gap between body and disconnected sound closed in, her head buzzed. Her eyes opened, unfocused.

"This is Angela. Angela Wise." She heard a woman's panicked voice. She thought she detected a hint of admiration as well, which confused her. And that name, Angela, sounded foreign. Did it belong to her?

"Oh my God. It is. It is." A man's voice. She noticed panic in his tone. She could not see; her head was flush with the ground, and she did not try to move it. She simply noted the voices surrounding her; the murmurings of considerate cicadas—muffled but encompassing her being.

"She's famous! It's Angela Wise!" The voices seemed to close in on her. She tried to focus, but her surroundings were enmeshed with the hazy blur of her vision.

"Call the ambulance," someone screamed.

"We got a bad scene here. That's Ms. Wise." Someone's voice grew closer as it brushed against her eardrum, it was so loud, and seemed to crack her head in half.

"Are you ok?" a deep voice asked.

Angela attempted to reply, but all she managed was a weak "ahhh."

"Someone call an ambulance." Another voice piped. Although she could not remember her own name, at least she knew and could distinguish between a man's voice and a woman's.

"We don't need an ambulance. Everyone calm down. She's fine." The same deep voice. It was firm and steady, authoritative.

"What's with you? Driving like a maniac! You didn't see the girl?" someone asked.

"I'm a doctor. I was on my way to the hospital where I have admitting privileges. I'll take her there," the deep voice said. Angela heard shuffling noises before the same voice continued. "Let me see that badge."

"*Dr. Michael Davis, MD. Primary Care Division-Gracie Square Hospital.* Alright, yeah, I can dig it."

"Wha's that?" another voice called.

"Aight. We got a doctor here, guys, make way! Let 'im do his job. Come on, out the way," Angela felt her body lifted off the ground, she couldn't speak or move. Someone carried her and placed her onto a leathery surface. Maybe the back seat of the man's car.

"Don't worry, Ms. Wise, I'm going to get you some help soon. I will take good care of you. Don't you worry." Angela wished she could put a face to the voice. She wanted to say something, but her body gave her words no chance, and they remained soundless in her mind. The world turned pitch black again.

WHO IS WHO?

ANGELA

"There, there, Ms. Wise. Is this better?" The familiar voice broke through the fog. But this time it was different, almost delicate. She felt something cold against her forehead. Her will, her need for answers allowed her—with much effort—to open her eyes. There was a man smiling before her He was tall and broad-shouldered with a mop of dark hair and heavy, solemn brows which were offset by a boyish grin. A pair of eyes the color of sea glass gleamed behind square-framed glasses that slipped down his long nose. She noticed a slight slit above the bridge of his nose, and it almost looked like another eye, a yellow one. She calmed herself, convinced she had imagined it and closed her eyes. When she reopened them, the same sea glass eyes stared back at her. The person had all the same features of the man—eyes, glasses, brows, and hair. But it was not a man. It was a woman.

"What's happening?"

"You need your rest girl, after such a big hit, your mind can wander far, convince your eyes of crazy things."

"What happened?" Angela managed. She tried to put her palm on her forehead, but the woman forced it away.

"You were in an accident. I'm here to make sure you'll recover from it." When she spoke, there were odd fluctuations in her voice: soft, then deep, then soft again.

"Oh, thank you, but I need-I need... I gotta go. She moved the ice pack the woman held to her forehead and stood. This was a mistake. She was so dizzy, the room blurred and spun around her. Angela fell back to the couch. "Where am I?"

No answer. She looked around and noted the small dark living room with one table and chair. She was sitting on a couch riddled with holes and that reeked of cigar smoke.

"You're still dizzy. You need to give it at least ten more minutes. Just lay back down and relax, Ms. Wise."

"Ms. Wise? That's my name?" she asked. She found the ice pack on the edge of the couch and pressed it back to her forehead.

"Of course. You are the best crime scene reporter New York City has ever seen. I was able to collect some of your paperwork after the accident." She pointed to the floor, where papers rested on a filthy green carpet.

Those pages meant nothing. They didn't have a place in Angela's world.

"Wait." Angela managed to stand up. "I don't recall any of this." Her breath caught in her lungs, hesitant to come out. "I am Angela Wise?" she plopped back down on the couch.

The stranger took a step closer. "You are even more beautiful in person than on television."

Angela shifted uncomfortably. She wanted out. She *needed* to get out of there.

"Don't be afraid," the woman said, "I'm trying to help you."

"I don't remember a thing," Angela confessed. She didn't know what else to do or who else would help her.

"Well, you're lucky that I'm a doctor." She took another step closer.

"Let me take a look." The woman placed her hands on either side of Angela's face and continued to stare straight into her eyes. The skin of her hands was rough—those of a working, blue-collar woman. Not a doctor.

No, no, Angela thought. *Something isn't right about this woman.* She tried to shake the woman's hands off. "I think I need to go to the hospital."

"You are scared, I see that. After what happened to you, you are shaken up, but I will take safe care of you now. Don't you worry about that. So beautiful." Her eyes had a dangerous glow. And that thing above the bridge of her nose was pulsating. Angela had not imagined it. The woman's glasses fell back to the tip of her nose.

The combination of her kidnapper's grip on her shoulder and Angela's weakness dampened, if not abolished, her ability to escape.

"What are you doing? Let me go!" Angela demanded.

Angela sat as far upright as she could, but the woman pushed her in the middle of her chest. Angela's back landed on the cushions of the couch, causing another dizzy spell.

The woman held Angela's hands down, and in a flash, Angela felt the woman's heavy body atop of her own. The woman's glasses fell off her long nose, but she didn't seem to care. Angela tried to wiggle out of the tight grip, but the woman kept her grasp. Her body felt heavier as her hands found Angela's neck.

"You belong to us. You understand? *Us.*"

"Let me go! Let go of me!" She panicked as she tried to fight her way out. She felt weak, but she kept fighting. Her fingers located long locks of dark hair and yanked them as hard as they could.

The captor remained unaffected. Angela ended up with only a handful of dry, brittle hair. She threw it on the floor and dug nails into the woman's skin. She tried to tear at that flesh but found that it was nothing like human skin. It was smooth and hard as a polished opal.

The kidnapper looked at Angela, and it was a look she barely recognized. Angry and insane admiration. Crazed and hungered.

"You're so beautiful, girl. We all want to be this beautiful, but it is not our time. Not until we have you. Your hair." She inhaled and said things that made even less sense. "The smell of Blood River. Your eyes are brighter than any Ortor. You are perfect."

While the woman was in her sick trance, Angela screamed for help.

She screamed as she twisted beneath the woman's body weight. She couldn't remember ever having been attacked. She couldn't recall much at all. As she realized that she couldn't fight any longer, Angela felt a massive hand cover her mouth. The skin tasted sour. Something slimy crawled from her triceps up to her neck. The writhing slime traced around her eyes and nose.

Maggots. They crawled out of the holes in the couch. Angela felt sick, and she opened her mouth to scream again, but that bitter hand covered her mouth, forbidding the scream.

Her eyes followed the fingers of the appendage and she saw that it had a green slime coating its dry bumps. She felt a warm drop of saliva land on her cheek and looked back to her kidnapper's eyes. The woman looked almost satisfied as she tightened her hands around Angela's neck. Angela tried to fight with whatever strength she had left. She kicked as she grabbed at the smooth surface of the woman's back and tried to find any location with give, somewhere she could sink her nails in and hurt the woman.

During the few minutes of her struggle, she accomplished only a loss of energy.

"We are not allowed to be so close to you yet, you know. But I could not help it, I had to see for myself that you were real."

That was the last thing Angela heard the woman say. There was something... pulsating above the bridge of the woman's nose. The skin pulsed until a slit appeared, and another eye—a yellow one—ripped the slit open as it appeared.

Angela's hands fell to the side and her legs went limp. She closed her eyes. If she couldn't fight reality, at the very least, she could block it out.

☙❧

"Are you ok?" a soft voice inquired. Angela opened her eyes, kicked her feet, and swung her arms as she regained consciousness. She was on a couch again, but it was different. This one smelled of fresh lavender, and it was clean. The apartment looked almost identical to the last one as far as the layout was concerned, but it housed fresh flowers, stunning furnishings, and vibrant colors. Even so, she was terrified.

"Get away!" she screamed, holding up her fists.

"Oh! No, no, no worries. The cops are on their way. How are you feeling?"

"I... I don't know" she replied, loosening her fists. The man in front of her was tall and slender. His hair was a light brown with a hint of red. He had perfectly styled it and combed it to the side, but Angela could make out a few strands of curls behind his ears. "Confused." Though her whole body ached, she managed to sit.

"You're fine now, you poor girl, I was able to get to you before..." he trailed off, clearing his throat, "before that maniac could get to you, in ways we wouldn't want him to." He handed her a tall glass of cool water. "Here, drink this," he half-commanded as he paced the room.

"Thanks. Wait, *him*? No. The person who did this to me was not a man. It was a woman." she took a drink of the water. "It all happened so fast."

"It's ok now. You're safe, but I understand if you don't trust me yet. I get it. And you must have been in shock. But that was a man. He lives just over there—he's my neighbor. He moved in here a few months ago. Definitely a guy. Got him locked up in that filthy apartment of his. Tied up his puny hands and feet. One hell of a voice you got there, girlie. That psycho didn't hurt you as much as he could've."

"B-but I fought *her*. *Her* hair was in my hands. *Her* voice, was what I heard... her..." Angela stopped herself when she noticed him look at her as if she were a stray cat searching for someone to take her in, to love her, to believe in her.

A man shoved me into his car... she thought. *Right?* The memory was hazy at best. If it was even real. *What happened? Was I imagining the woman?* Angela curled up into herself and took shallow breaths.

This new stranger sighed, but not in a frustrated way. More like he was worried for her. "Take another sip and try to relax." After she finished drinking, he picked up her cup. "I knew something was up with that cat. Always seemed a little off, you know what I mean? He won't be going anywhere until the cops get here." The man continued to travel the same line back and forth across the room.

"Thank you," she mumbled, taking a deep breath. "Can you please stop doing that? The pacing? I'm still dizzy."

He stopped right away. "Sorry. It's a habit."

"It-it's ok. I shouldn't... I shouldn't have..." Angela stuttered, trying to find the right words. "Who should I be thanking for saving me from that monster?"

"Oh. Me? Liam—pleased to meet you." He held out his hand.

Angela hesitated to shake it. Instead, she retreated into the couch. "Thank you again, Liam, for saving me. My name is..." she couldn't say it. She could not remember what that awful woman, or as Liam corrected, *man* had called her.

"Angela. Angela Wise. You're like, a movie star. Being the first renowned woman reporter. That was something else. Far out, you know? Society accepting a woman in a man's role."

Liam picked up a glass, filled it with ice and water, and offered it to Angela.

"Maybe people will realize that we're all equal. Don't you hate how they put everyone in compartments and sort them out on shelves based on what label we're supposed to have. And if you fall off your shelf, you're banned from *their* store. Their norm?" Liam shook his head and waved his hands. "I'm rambling, but you know, those people who dictate what's acceptable—the rules—those don't have to be the rules. Anyway, your journalism skills are marvelous. That neighbor of mine must have had some kinda crazy obsession with you. I'm sure many others do too, but that floor-wipe.... How did he manage to get the one and only Angela Wise into his flimsy apartment anyway?"

"She—sorry, I mean, *he*—said he was a doctor and was going to help me after the accident."

Liam scoffed. "He's not a doctor. He's an unemployed creep." Angela looked at her feet. "The cops should be here any second. I'm gonna go check on that the jerk. Hope he knows what's coming to him. Rub it in his face." Liam headed for the entrance to his apartment.

"I'm coming with you." Angela stood, and to her surprise, the man accepted her company.

They crossed the hall and opened the door. But after a search of the place, no one was there. A mist of dark purple smoke hung in the air.

Liam's face contorted. "What in the world? How did he escape?"

"Liam, I don't know what's happening. Or going on. Can I confess something?" She didn't wait for him to answer before she continued, "I don't remember anything. I don't know how I ended up at-at... his place. I don't remember anything."

"Come on, we gotta take you to a real doctor. You could have a concussion. Loss of memory? We have to take you to the hospital, and we have to do it fast."

That day, Angela decided that she hated doctors, in addition to men and women with long noses and glasses.

JULIA

Winter
Late 1930s

I want you to know that, even if it seemed otherwise—I've always loved you. I've loved you every second of every day. I have done some terrible things, but through all of my actions, I always held the image of your innocent eyes in my mind and in my heart.

— A LETTER

Julia wrapped her thin arms around her waist and drew her knees closer to her chest. The holes in her rags offered little protection from the blistering winds of the January morning. The city's almost empty blocks would flood with New York's careless citizens in less than twenty minutes.

She squinted into the distance. A tall figure approached her block, but it wasn't who she was waiting for. Who she was always waiting for. She would have recognized his curly auburn hair from a mile away. Even when he wore a hat, his curls branched out in all sorts of directions. As the blonde-haired passerby neared, she freed her arms to pluck her dirty cup from the pavement of the block corner.

"Oh please, kind sir, can you spare some change?"

The stranger stopped. For a moment, Julia's heart alighted with hope. She tightened her grip on the cup, waiting to see him reach into his pocket, waiting to hear the coins hit the empty bottom.

"I'm nothing but a shadow to you, kind sir. But please help. I have nothing to eat."

A nasty frown spread across the stranger's face. "You scag grifter," he said. He looked down at her, lowering his head to spit in her cup. "Get yourself up and find a job." The man stormed away.

Julia used the corner of her tattered shirt to wipe the saliva away, and she held back the tears she so often wanted to release.

One lonely snowflake landed on her nose and then another. A bit of snow collected on the navy-blue sign, slightly covering the white letters reading *BROADWAY* and 42nd *STREET*.

People hurried past her without a glance. Humanity was intolerable. No one was kind enough to spare a penny. She searched for the only one who looked her way, for the kind smile. But she didn't see his red, messy locks amid the crowd. She glanced to her right, wondering if he would cross her path that frosty morning. He had to. He had been passing by on this block for as long as she could remember.

He'd served as one of her few distractions from the chill of the streets, from the chill of people's hearts. Her other distraction was reading. Books taught her things she couldn't learn on the street. She loved reading about art, history, science; but mostly, she loved Jane Austen. Romance. She tried to visit the library as often as her feet would carry her there. She read any book she could pluck from the shelves before the librarians kicked her out. She was content with picking up discarded newspapers and anything else she could get her hands on. Her most dedicated teacher... written words. She was grateful for all of them. She was proud of the education she made for herself, but that still didn't land her a job or favor in other people's eyes. That's because she was a "dirty scum," as most called her. When she would curl up next to the lion statues at the New York Public Library, she would envision herself living in worlds more fantastical than her own. Those worlds were one of the very few things that helped Julia cope with her life.

Her stomach rumbled, reminding her of its emptiness. As more snow accumulated by her feet, she formed a tiny ball and cupped it in her hands. It took a few moments for it to melt in her chilled palms, and when it did, she lifted her palms to her cracked lips, shivering as the frigid liquid traveled down her esophagus.

Laughter floated from down the street, catching her ear and her attention. She squinted against the sun to see where the happy sound was coming from. A little girl skipped cheerfully between her parents, each clutching one of her hands. The girl looked to be all of seven years old. Julia's chest tightened as she recalled her own seventh birthday—the last memory she had of her parents. They'd gifted her a beautiful, silver heart locket. But nearly everything after that day—every place in her mind where memories should live—was blank. She wished she knew more about her parents, or how she ended up on these streets. Many of her days and nights were spent wondering—trying to piece together a past that had vanished from her mind.

"Good morning," called a familiar deep voice, interrupting her wistful thoughts.

Her eyes traveled to meet his gaze. His dark blues beamed with kindness and magnificence.

"Morning to you," she managed, swallowing the rest of the ice water. She couldn't help but smile, though she was all nerves. The cold wasn't the only thing making her tremble.

Snowflakes fell from his messy curls as he lowered himself to drop change into her empty cup. The smell of fresh cologne and cigars took her to a place beyond the streets. To somewhere happy and peaceful. She imagined how much taller he would be standing next to her. How proud she would be to walk with her arm in his.

Men like him didn't mingle with beggars, and if they decided to, they were viewed as some kind of victim. By the time she came back to the cold reality of the present, the kind stranger was already moving on. "Thank you… friend," she whispered into the whipping wind. His back muscles shifted beneath the thick fabric of his jacket as he crossed the street and made a right on East 53rd.

Her eyes trailed him until she could no longer see the swaying of his long dark coat. He reminded her of a hero. Scant opportunities arose to pass time, so she often imagined the thoughtful man as her very own knight in shining armor. In her fantasies, he'd swoop in one day and rescue her from the streets. He'd whisk her away to somewhere clean, warm, and safe. Later they'd drink hot cocoa and sit by the Hudson, laughing and chatting about their days.

Eventually, the streets—which had recently bustled with the influx of men hurrying to get to work—slowly ground to a halt. She pulled herself from the cold concrete and picked up her belongings. Hoping the police wouldn't kick her out of the station, she crossed the street toward the Q train.

Somewhat comfortable on the station's chilly steps, she managed to count the change in her cup. She cupped the coins close to her chest they clinked against one another. Fifty cents. Enough for a couple days' worth of food, maybe three if she spent the money wisely.

"Watch'a doin' in my spot?" The voice of Eddie, her drunkard acquaintance, shattered her joy.

She wrapped her fingers tightly around the spare change. He always managed to sniff her out whenever she had a little money.

"Getting comfortable so I can hopefully survive the first winter night of the year," she replied, wishing she could punch his red face.

"Nope. No. You know damn well this be my spot."

"Don't see your name on it. I was here first." She wanted to defend her little space in the covered threshold. But Ed was the only person she somewhat got along well with on the streets, so picking a fistfight with him was off the table.

The short, bald drunkard swayed from side to side, trying to keep his balance. "I say, get up, girl. Befo' I make a scene an' none of us gets it."

"For old-times' sake, be a friend and let me have this spot," Julia pleaded.

"Friend or foe, I gotta keep me warm too."

"Stop being difficult. There's another station a block away. Go there because I'm not leaving this spot," she said, banging her cup on the concrete.

"Cop's be raidin' the other stations. I've been to almost all of 'em already. This is the best spot, an' you know that." He looked down at her cup. "Is that money I heard comin' from that cup o' yours?"

"No. that was your wild, wino, imagination," she said, hiding the cup behind her.

"C'mon. Share some change. I got nothin' for today."

"Why should I share it with you? You'll just spend it on booze, anyway. So, *no*."

"I gotta eat too, lil' lady."

"Stop spending on booze."

Ed's red face turned a brighter crimson. He swayed his arms as if readying for a fight. "Get outta my spot, lil' lady."

Julia didn't budge. "I'll freeze to death out there tonight."

"Then spare some change, and you get the spot."

She looked down at her torn shoes and her stockings filled with holes. She reached for her cup and offered him ten cents.

"I ain't no butter-and-egg man, ya know. If you wan' this spot, you gotta do betta' than that, lil' lady. I might have ta sleep out there."

"Fine. Hand me that scarf, and you'll get more."

He tucked his scarf into his undersized jacket. "Hell no. I may be a bit woozy, but I know how to hold me own."

"You're such a pill. Just get out of here," she handed him another ten cents. "Shake a leg, get me something to eat, too. I will not risk losing this spot after paying such expensive rent."

Ed smoothed the top of his scarf. "Will be back in a zippy," he said with a crooked smile.

THE CLUES

ANGELA
Spring
Early 1970s

This letter exists so that you can have access to knowledge—knowledge I didn't hold until it was too late. You come from a family with a unique lineage. You are what is known as an Ortor. Surely, by now, you've encountered things that cannot be explained by either sense or science. Those things are due to your bloodline, which possesses magical abilities to leverage against great evils. Ortors are often volatile beings because they do not understand their own powers, which leaves them vulnerable to the evil they should know to fight against...

— A LETTER

"Thank you for coming with me," Angela said.

"Listen, it's ok. We are all mixed in with each other, like a stew, in the same pot of life. If we don't help one another, we might as well evaporate into our own egos. I would rather evaporate from the ego pot and help a few people. Without anything in return. You know?"

Liam stood while Angela looked around.

The doctor's office seemed cold. The walls were plain white, there were no other patients in the waiting room, and Angela found herself annoyed by the cheerfulness of the secretary. Angela folded and unfolded the newspaper, reading its contents as though she could find her life details inside. Maybe there were details inside it that would help her memory function again.

"Coffee?" Liam stood before her with a large cup of steaming liquid. "I wasn't sure if you like it with sugar or milk or... well, here it is anyway."

"I don't know if I like coffee. I mean, I know what it *is*. But I don't remember the taste."

"Ms. Wise. The doctor will see you now." The sing-song voice of the secretary projected well across the room. Angela wanted to roll her eyes. How can someone be so happy when they see so many miserable people enter the office?

She followed the nurse into the doctor's office. It was cold, or maybe she was in shock. Maybe it was both. After the doctor introduced himself, he asked her a series of questions.

The doctor continued explaining to Angela that she was suffering from "RA," or Retrograde Amnesia resulting from trauma. A "post-traumatic amnesia," he called it.

"The good news," he said, "is your procedural memory is intact. That is the part of your long-term memory, responsible for remembering how to do things. Things such as normal daily tasks: like tying your shoelaces, riding a bike, or driving a car without consciously thinking about how you are doing it. The bad news is that you have loss of episodic events. But those too can be triggered—reignited if you will— by living your daily life. Take care not to overwork your physical or mental processes. Take it easy until you regain your memories. I want to see you back in the office for a follow up in two weeks."

Angela lowered her eyes to the floor. The frustration was immense, and that feeling alone nearly sparked something, some phantom of a memory, but she couldn't quite reach it. Whenever she picked her brain for information, it failed her. She pushed herself to remember anything, but it was like she'd found a large heavy rock blocking a road. And she was pushing it out of the way all by herself. And it rocked a bit, it rolled a bit, but it always resettled.

"Doctor, is it possible with this form of amnesia, to hallucinate, or something of that nature? As in seeing something that's not there, or mixing people up?" Angela shifted in her chair; she didn't want to sound crazy, so she whispered, "or even mix up places?"

"That is highly unlikely. You may be confused, but hallucinate? No." The doctor scribbled something in his chart. "Are you experiencing any hallucinations, Angela?"

"No, no. Just curious about the whole thing, that's all. And confused."

When she was done with the doctor, she met Liam back in the waiting hall.

Liam walked behind Angela to the elevator, down to street level and into a cab. The drive through the city to Liam's apartment was short in distance but felt longer than it should have. The two discussed what her diagnosis was, and her prognosis.

"Well, at least the doctor said it's not a severe case. It's not long term, and you should get your memories back if you just live your life, right?" Liam said, opening his apartment door.

"How am I supposed to go back living my lifestyle? I don't even remember my original lifestyle... I have nothing to go back to. I don't know what to go back to. Right now, I don't know anybody. Except for you," Angela said, her voice shaking.

"Well, you don't have to go anywhere right now. You can stay here until we figure out where you live."

Angela hesitated to walk inside, but she had no idea where else to go.

"Ok," he said, likely sensing her discomfort. "If you prefer, you can rent a hotel room across the street, and we can get to figuring out your story in the morning."

"That sounds good," she said. "And thank you for not disclosing the full story to the police. If I'm famous, I wouldn't want this all over the news. I'm going to head across the street."

"Don't forget these." He handed Angela the stack of papers that the woman, or man, who attacked her had pointed out to her.

She scanned through the messy pile. "Looks like I was working on a big story."

"May I?" Liam extended his hands. Angela handed the papers back.

She noticed how his eyebrows lifted as he skimmed the pages. A hint of surprise, maybe even hope, flashed in his green eyes.

"Fascinating," he said, scratching his head. Still engrossed in the papers, he walked to his couch and sat as he continued to read. Angela stood like a statue outside the door. Liam seemed to forget she was there.

"Look at this," he exclaimed, "It looks like you were investigating the death of a billionaire. Jack Roe." Liam's voice broke a little. Angela looked from the door to the man holding her work, and she took a seat next to him.

"I wish I was as excited as you are about this." Her lips curled into a frown.

"You have to be. If you want to remember, you have to jump right back on the wagon."

"Billionaire? Jack Roe? Who was he?"

Liam shook his head and swept one page after the next, skimming their contents. "Angela, this case was dropped years ago by the authorities—no one knows what happened to Mr. Roe. But according to your paperwork, it seems like you had a pretty good lead."

Angela felt more confused. "I don't understand any of this. it's all too much."

"I'll help you. I promise. I can even help you with this story."

"The story is the last thing on my mind now."

"You're right. I'm sorry. You need to get rest."

"Why would you want to help me, anyway?"

"I knew a bit about the Roe's and have a special interest in your story. I don't... I don't really want to overwhelm you right now. With, you know, your memory, so can we leave it at that for now?"

"It is a bit much. I would like to know where I come from and who I am first. Before I start worrying about other stuff. But the only help I need at this point is figuring out where I come from and remembering something—anything about my life."

"I'll help you, if you'll let me. I mean, I'll do my best. There's like this saying that if you save someone, they're your responsibility."

"Liam, I'm not your responsibility. I can't thank you enough, but you don't need to do—"

"Let me rephrase, then. I want to help you. If you want me to."

Her head was throbbing. She couldn't shake the events from earlier, and she desperately wished to remember her life. Her mind was a void —it was like a blank sheet of paper. She wanted to scream under the weight of all she did not know. She didn't know if she had ever loved or had a family; she didn't know where she lived; she didn't know how she felt about herself. She had looked in the mirror earlier in the hospital, and Liam showed her a newspaper clip with one of her stories and her picture. She was pretty and successful, and people seemed to like her, but that did not bring her comfort. Strangely, she felt comfortable with Liam. Which was a wonderful thing, as he was the only person she knew.

Liam placed the papers on the coffee table and walked to the kitchen. He came back with two cups of hot tea.

Angela stared at her tea as she swirled the liquid in her cup, then she broke the silence. "I'll allow it. Can I trust you?"

Liam smiled. She smiled back. She decided to take a chance—to allow herself to trust him. He'd only been kind and helpful to her. The hours they'd already spent together had helped forge a bond between them, and she could feel that bond growing as the hours ticked by.

"What about you? I'm sure you have a job or... or something? I don't want to take you from your daily routine. You shouldn't sacrifice your life to help me recall mine, I suppose, is what I'm trying to say."

"I own an antique dealership. My clients work with me on my time— on my schedule. Even if I take a few days off, they'd never trade my expertise for anyone else's." Liam punctuated his statement by waving his hand in the air, placing one leg across the other, while sipping his tea.

"Do you have any family?" Angela asked.

"Yes. An older brother and a younger sister. I haven't seen them in a while though. Been busy with work. They don't live too far from Long Island."

"Long Island..." Angela trailed off, imagining a skyscape. *Long Island.* She could recall landmarks, yet not any personal details about herself. It was odd, at best. "I wonder if I have any family." She leaned forward and placed her mug on the table.

"Tomorrow we'll go down to the news station, look into your employee files, and get your address. We can get your emergency contact information. We'll go from there."

"Sounds like a plan. I'm not sure If I would want anyone at work finding out that I have amnesia." She sighed, frustrated beyond her own. "How I hope my memories come back!"

"Me too. Look, maybe even if you can't remember yet, but if you're up for it, of course, we can continue working on the case you started," Liam said, looking hopeful. "I think it was important to you, and it could tell you more about who you are."

Angela took a deep breath. The colorful clock hanging above a small bookshelf reminded her of the flowers she'd seen by the hospital entrance. She picked at her barren memory for a snapshot of similar flowers, but the slate was still blank.

It was close to midnight, and Angela was exhausted. She turned to Liam, who was already snoring on the couch. She walked across the room to the pink loveseat, grabbed one of the throw blankets, and covered him. Once she had positioned herself comfortably on one of the recliners, she, too, fell into a deep restful sleep.

❦

The strong smell of coffee woke her. Liam walked into the room carrying two cups and breakfast sandwiches on a plate painted with daisies.

Angela sat up. "Thank you. I'm sorry I stayed here. You fell asleep, and it was too late for me to walk over to the hotel."

"Nonsense," Liam said, smiling. Angela took the cup in her hands. After resting, she felt a little better. She was able to take in her surroundings and retain them this time. The living room was perfectly designed and very neat. The sofa was dotted with light blue pillows, which matched the drapes. He had a few green plants, and small decorative dwarf palm trees situated at each corner of the window. There were mirrors, at the front door and by the dining room table surrounded by large and colorful picture frames. The whole apartment was a color parade, but with style and elegance. The coffee table displayed scented candles, and they mesmerized her.

"The candles," she pointed out.

"Oh. these little things. I love scented candles and oils," he said.

"It's just when I look at them, my mind feels like's it's shrinking, like I should be remembering something, but I just can't. It's like an on-the-tip-of-my-tongue kinda thing. I... um... I *almost* know what I want to know. I mean about the candles, but when I try to remember, I can't."

"Scent is strongly associated with memory. At least, I think those are the rumors I've heard. Don't worry too much, Angela. The doctor said it will take time. Take it easy."

"Thank you for being so generous. And for being such a gentleman. I suppose there are only a select few men you can trust these days."

"You don't have to worry about me that way." He looked at Angela, with his striking, kind deep green eyes. She noticed a hint of blue in them, and that spot of blue seemed to wash over the green when he was happy.

"You know you can trust me, right? Well, can I trust you?" The muscles in his jawline tensed.

"I think so. I mean, I think I'm a trustworthy person."

"The truth is... I'm not into women. So..." He took another sip of his coffee. His face once again serious but this time Angela noticed sadness too. "Our society is so brutal about gays," he said. "It's very hard to find someone you can be yourself with and trust."

"I wish they weren't so brutal. But I won't be. I like men, too, you know? I think..." Angela paused to think about this. "I do. So, we have something in common."

Liam cleared his throat. "Thank you. Now, are you ready to tackle the day?"

"I sure am."

"The news station it is. When we get there, just act natural. As you said, you don't want them to know you don't remember anything, otherwise, they might take you off the job, and we need their resources to investigate the disappearance of Jack Roe. Perhaps later we can tell them. Your co-workers might be able to help with your memories."

"Right. I don't think I want them to take me off the job. I need to live my life as much as possible, and judging by all this paperwork, my life was my job." She was frustrated that she had no idea how to do that job, but she just hoped it would work out. It was the best she could do.

They called a cab and went straight for the studio. It was located on a busy street that Angela didn't recognize. In her mind, the city was a foreign place. Another empty space. The studio was also new and fresh. She had to think about how to navigate the building while acting natural.

THE CELLAR

ANGELA

"Angie. Angie." A heavy-set young man ran toward them as soon as he spotted them walking into the studio. Waving at Angela, his red cheeks puffed up like a well-fed hamster. An ID badge was hanging over his neck which read "Robert: Camera Crew."

"The whole station was looking for you! It's not like you to be late. Everyone was worried sick!" He dropped his hands to the side. "What happened to you yesterday? You were supposed to cover for John. They had the weatherman do it, and George the Bull wasn't happy about that one, you know what I mean?"

She tried not to panic. Tried to look apologetic instead of insecure—she had known these people. She *did* know these people. Somewhere. She didn't want to alarm them. What if her condition could cause her to lose her job? She didn't know how forgiving anyone at this place was. She couldn't remember. "I'm so sorry. I... I had an emergency."

"George is in production six now. I'm sure he'll come down his piss ladder when he sees you. And what emergency?" He scratched the back of his head.

"Excuse us." Liam stepped in, fixing his hat. "Your name?"

"Robert. The man behind the camera," he said proudly, stretching out his porky hand to greet Liam, "And who might you be?"

Liam refused his hand. "I'm Liam. I am a friend accompanying Angela for a trip to her office. Excuse us." Liam squeezed past him.

"Wrong way, buddy. It's to the left," Robert shouted after him.

"That's right, Liam, the other way." Angela followed Robert's lead. She wished that she could trust Robert; tell him and everyone else she worked with about the accident, what happened, and what she needed. But she didn't know Robert, or George, or John. For now, she was comfortable with her decision to keep her amnesia a secret.

"Sorry Robert, but I have to go." She waved and yelled back.

Once they were inside her office, Liam took the liberty of sifting through all the drawers. After a moment, he waved a piece of paper in the air. "Angela, look. I found something. Apparently, your home address is on Long Island, and you have an address listed right here in the city." Liam flipped through the pages. "Here's your emergency contact. It's... Edward Bile. We should probably call him. I mean, this is what he's there for, right?"

Angela stopped to think, or to not think. Things seemed to be happening too fast, and information arrived at the speed of lightning. She rubbed her eyes and took a deep breath.

"Let's visit the apartment first. We'll call this Edward from there. I mean, it's an emergency, I suppose, but I don't want to have to pretend to know this guy. I don't want to hurt a person's feelings when I don't know who they are to me. Should I do it that way?" Angela blurted all her thoughts as she pulled her employee file from Liam's hands.

Robert peeked in. "What are you up to?"

"None of your business," Liam snapped. He turned back to what he was doing, put his hat back on and shoved the file inside his coat pocket.

"It *is* my business. Angie has lots of work to do. She's about to crack a big case, which means we'll have a nice, big story."

"Sorry, Robert." Angela touched his shoulder. She then figured that she probably never put a finger on him before, because he stopped breathing for a second, disbelief painted on his face. The way his round cheeks got red when he looked at her, and the way his lips trembled when he spoke her name seemed to confirm her suspicion. Angela and Liam looked at one another then took off toward the door. Angela glanced back to ensure Robert wasn't following them.

⬥

The small apartment was cozy. Paintings depicting sun-kissed scenery, and oceans breathed life into the walls and air of the place. Although her surroundings brought her some measure of calm, they failed to trigger any memories. Next to a window sat a small table, stacked high with more papers and a half empty coffee mug. The layout was open so she could see the living room from the kitchen. She had a couch, a coffee table, plants, more paintings, and a plush rug. She wanted to sink into the couch and cover herself with a soft blanket, close her eyes and sleep forever. The apartment smelled like sweet oranges and old ink. Even in the living room, there were papers, newspaper clippings, and books cluttering the space. They were on the coffee table, the edge of the couch, and even the rug.

"All I see here are papers on top of papers, and files on top of files. If this was my work, it must not have been easy. I don't know how I'll sort this out," Angela said. She wanted to at least pretend to work on her project because the ability to actively do so was caged somewhere within her brain. Even if a beginning point was unclear. Angela hoped that if she began, her body would take over automatically. Muscle memory. She was banking on the autopilot within her.

"Do you remember any of this? Is it helping?" Liam asked.

Angela plucked a book from an end table and flipped through it. The smell was familiar and while it gave her a small rush of excitement, no concrete attachments to them arose. "No," she said, slapping the book back onto the table with a little too much force,

"Ok. Let's keep looking. Who knows what could help?" Liam reassured her.

Angela inspected her not-so-neat apartment. It looked more like an office than a living space. "How did I live here? Looks like I'm a workaholic."

"Yeah, well, I wouldn't be surprised to know that," Liam said as he sifted through Angela's personal file. "Ah!" he exclaimed. "Here. This is Edward's number." Liam handed her the paper with her emergency contact.

She went to the rotary phone in the corner—that was good. She knew where the phone was... somehow. She didn't have to look. Some of her instincts remained intact, but the confusion remained. She tried the number and hung up on the twenty-seventh ring. She shrugged and shot Liam a look that begged for help.

"Let's drive out to Long Island and see if anything triggers your memory there," he suggested.

They jotted down an address that correlated with Long Island, then left the apartment, taking a short cab ride back to Liam's. Once there, they decided to forgo the cabs and take Liam's car. They rode in silence. Angela looked out the window, trying to relax. She took deep breaths. The scenery changed from busy hustle city streets and tall buildings to tall trees and greenery.

They pulled up to a mansion. "This is it," Liam said, putting the car in park. "Should be your primary residence."

Angela was in awe at the sprawling estate before them. It seemed like something brand new and alien. But this was, supposedly, her home.

Liam's eyebrows raised. "As an antique dealer, I can tell you this home is marvelous, and I cannot wait to see the inside." Liam clapped his hands, then hurriedly opened his door. Angela saw how he glowed with anticipation when he opened the passenger door to let her out of the car. "After you, madam."

She stepped out, trying to remember something—anything. The tall untrimmed grass and trees on both sides of the C-shaped driveway gave a feeling of emptiness. Angela averted her attention to the grounds after noting the unkempt vines that crept up the house. At least something living had taken it up, just not a person.

"I'm sure I have the keys with me," she said. When she dug through her purse, her fingers brushed against the cold metal of a serrated key. She was surprised to discover the many keys on her key ring, and she did not know which one belonged to the house. She tried ten or so before one fit and turned the lock. She swung the double doors open with ease.

Before them lay a grand floor of white marble tiles, which sprouted white pillars, and a grand spiral staircase. To their right was an entrance to a sprawling family room. At the very back of the living room was a door. It led to a library. To the right of the family room, was a large kitchen with a deck, overlooking the estate's garden. The kitchen opened to a dining room, and from there, a study room was easy to locate. There were more doors, more entrances to more rooms. They had seen so much already. And there was more to see upstairs.

Although it was orderly, everything had a thin layer of dust on it. The one large flowerpot at the entryway held a small, dead tree. Angela eagerly looked for family pictures—a great clue if there had been any. But the walls were empty. The fireplace was vacant of any kindling or even ashes. Angela shivered. It felt like a ghost house.

"Does anything look familiar?"

"No. I'll see if going upstairs will help."

"Do you mind if I explore down here? I just love the antiquity of this place!"

"Do your thing," Angela said, heading for the stairs.

As she ascended the spiral staircase, her head throbbed. It was sudden and quick. Like lightning passed over her brain and then disappeared. She saw herself as a little girl, running up and down those stairs. And a woman's harsh voice following behind her *"Stop this instant child! We have to practice the lightning spell."*

She stopped and looked around her, as though the woman was still there. It was an automatic response to something she felt was from the past, not present. The barren home reflected that—a past forgotten.

She hated feeling so out of control. Her head hurt, her heart raced, and she was angry. She felt shaky, first in her heart, then her head, as if her brain were being battered. No, it was not anger, not fully. She wanted to scream. She closed her eyes as the shaking worsened.

Then she heard the light noise of creaking and cracking. And although her eyes were shut, she was able to see as though she were in some kind of lucid dream. She saw all the doors upstairs close and open, one after another. But as much as she wanted to, she couldn't open her eyes, as though the lucid dream state led to sleep paralysis. She saw herself in a dark place, like a deep forest, but worse. The forest was rich with thick thorn-like trees that branched out in pointy spikes, blocking the view of the stick-laden path before her. The thorns resembled both wood and metal. She saw herself pinch her nose to avoid the smell of rot. It was like she was watching herself from an omniscient perspective while having a first-person perspective simultaneously—she existed in two places at once. She felt something on her left shoulder, and she jerked back. But the other Angela, did not. It was a green snake, staring at her.

And then she was back upstairs, the strange (but less strange) reality flooded her mind and vision.

❧

Liam explored the living room quarters, in obvious and loud awe of the paintings, drapery, and most of all, by the Victorian white and gold chaise.

"Angela!" He screamed, as he couldn't see her, "you should see this chaise, it's marvelous, it's beautiful, it's everything." Angela didn't reply, but that didn't matter to Liam now, because he had the chaise's company. He sat on it, and while caressing its fabric with a tender touch, he spoke to the chaise, as if speaking to a child:

"Oh, Antique Rococo Louis XVI Baroque Throne Settee Couch Chaise, White Leather, Original Gold Leaf Gild Frame Shabby Heavy Wood... you." he patted the couch, then stood to study the fabric of the cushions. Dusting them off, lifting one cushion then another.

"What a shame, leaving you in so much dust," he said to his new friend.

He noticed a paper tucked deep under the bare fabric. "Why would anyone tuck garbage in this beauty." With a shake of his head, he carefully placed one of the cushions on the floor.

He smoothed out and studied the paper. He was less certain that it was trash. "Hey, Angela? Can you come look at this?" *6982* was staring back at him. "I for sure think I found something."

"Found what?" a male's voice replied.

Liam shoved the paper into his pocket. Almost tumbling over the chaise, he found his balance and stood guard. "Who are you and what are you doing here?"

"I should ask ya the same," the strange man barked back, fixing his hat, and adjusting his tie.

⚜

Angela heard voices from downstairs. They weren't alone in the house, and Liam might need her help. She found a washroom and splashed water on her face. She was near the stairs now, watching the two men. "What's going on?" her voice broke the tension between Liam and the other man.

"Oh. Angela. I haven't seen ya in foreva'. I'm so glad ya back, is this young man with ya?"

"Yes, he is," Angela said, trying to keep her cool.

The man took off his hat and wiped sweat from his bald head.

"Saw a strange car parked outside an' decided to check on the house. It's been ages since anyone came by hea'."

Angela and Liam exchanged looks.

"We jus' spoke yesterday, an' ya didn' tell me ya comin' here. You tryn'a avoid me or somethin'?"

"No, no. Of course not," Angela replied. The man seemed offended at the idea that she was avoiding him, and while it could have been an act, she wanted to play it safe. This man might be a family member. Or a friend.

"Good. If you hear, it means ya decided to take a break. Good for ya. That story 'bout the missing man, Mr. Roe, that's stressin' ya out. Ya need time off?" He sounded casual, but it sounded forced. She was almost certain he was acting.

"I'm not sure yet," Angela replied. Liam stirred when he heard Mr. Roe's name.

The man took a deep breath. "Tell me, how ya been? I read many of youses articles, mus' say I'm impressed. Ya are a wonderful reporta'. I bet ya busy, but ya should still come an' visit more often, I know it mus' be hard when Zilda passed, but ya have me hea'."

Angela descended the stairs and stood next to Liam. She felt safer when she was close to him.

The man didn't seem to notice her discomfort. He took off his coat and freely walked into the kitchen, reached into one of the cabinets for a cup, and poured water from the sink. He then continued, adding extra enthusiasm to his manner of speaking.

"I wana' hear everythin'. Tell me about the career, 'bout ya new life. Is it everythin' ya eva' dreamed of?" he peeked out of the kitchen and gave Liam a stern look.

"Sorry I was a bit rude earlier, but I've neva' seen ya, and keepin' an eye on this kiddo hea' is my duty." He extended his hand to Liam. "I'm Edward Bile, but ya can call me Ed. I'm a friend of Angela's"

"And her emergency contact." Liam smiled. "It's very nice to meet you, Ed. We've been looking for you."

They went to the living room and made themselves comfortable. Angela and Liam sat on the chaise, and Edward sat on the couch. Angela then explained to him the events that led to their arrival at the mansion, and what they were hoping to accomplish by being there. Ed didn't interrupt, and by the end of their retelling of events, Angela was eager for him to take over the conversation.

She noted as confusion and a hint of fear crossed his eyes. The little spark he had in them when he'd first seen her was gone. He looked overly concerned. As if he was stuck on making a crucial decision.

"You look like you might need a drink," Liam cut in, bringing a bit of the spark back to Edwards's eyes.

"Right about now, I wish I had my ol' bottle." He took a deep breath, rubbing his hands together as if cleaning them with soap and water.

"Can't remember nothin', huh? Ok. I'll try to help. So, you lived hea' with your ma, Zilda, who was overprotective of you, and that's why you were homeschooled. You were awfully close to Zilda. You took good care of her. Befo' she passed away, she wanta' you to have the life you always wanta'. Like goin' to college and workin' as a reporter. She asked me for my real estate expertise, to help in buying you an apartment in the city." He put a handkerchief to his sweaty forehead and wiped it dry.

"To tell the truth—" Angela caught a flash of red in his cheeks and a little tremble in his lips when he said the word "truth." "I don' know too much 'bout youses family. We bumped into each otha' a few years back, and since then, we became sorta family friends, if ya dig?"

"Yeah. Thank you so much. That's helpful. I must have been devastated when my mother died," she said. She clasped her hands together tightly, desperately hoping to reignite any emotion. But she felt nothing. She decided to press Edward further. "So, you knew about my mother. Do you know anything about my father?" She felt he was keeping something from her. At the very least he looked nervous, so she figured there must have been more to his story.

Edward shrugged. "All I know is tha' he was a kind man, and he passed away, befo' ya were born."

Angela rose from the chaise, flung up her arms, then dropped them to her sides with a *slap*. "I'm not sure what to do with myself. Maybe I should stay here and try to remember. I could try looking at the rest of the house, see if anything feels or looks familiar." She walked into the kitchen. The void of the giant home gave her shivers. Everything looked carefully placed but it was lifeless, dusty, given up on, and lonely. It was like a black hole that had never seen, let alone housed, life itself.

"Great. You wanna stay hea'. This place needs a human in it," Ed called after her. He shook Liam's hand. "I gotta go, kids."

"I'm right aroun' the corna' if ya need me. Few houses down the block, numba' 2315." As soon as the door behind Ed closed, Liam ran to the kitchen and grabbed Angela's hand.

Angela rubbed her forehead with her free hand.

"You ok?"

"Yeah, just a headache, and confusion. Doctor did say confusion is possible after the accident."

"We'll get through this. Come on, I gotta show you something." Liam lowered his voice for the last part. Whispering like a child bursting at the seams to tell a secret.

"What is it?"

"I found this in the chaise." Liam fiddled in his pocket and pulled out a small piece of crumpled paper.

"Ok. What do you see in it?"

"The numbers. Look." He put the paper in front of Angela's face.

"Six-nine-eight-two," Angela read aloud.

"I think it's some sort of combination!" He gasped, looked around, then dashed from one room to another, leaving Angela open-mouthed in the living room. He looked like a maniac trying to find his way out of a fun-house maze. His hair was a mess. He must have visited every room on the first floor within a minute, even though it should certainly take longer. Angela supposed that finding strange numbers in a chaise lounge must have been too much for Liam to bear.

"According to my knowledge in the field, and this being a historical house—mansions like these usually have a cellar, with safes. I know without a doubt that there is a cellar here. And I also think this might be the code to the safe." Liam was back at her side, speaking with a total lack of modesty, and an inflated sense of authority. He scratched his bare chin as he speculated. "The cellar has to be somewhere in this house, maybe it was closed off? But why? That makes me want to find it even more."

"I see you've found yourself a mission." At this point, Angela was too tired to think or look for anything.

"I think I'll crash here overnight," she said rubbing her neck from exhaustion. "And then tomorrow I'll go back to the studio. Gotta figure out my daily routine so I can remember."

"Do you want me to stay?"

Angela yawned. "Please? I don't wanna be alone in this place. There sure are plenty of rooms, pick one to stay in." She started up the stairs, toward what she guessed was one of the bedrooms. "I'm going to lie down now. Goodnight Liam."

"Goodnight Angela."

She chose a delicately decorated but smaller room that boasted a light pink wall cover. She assumed this room must have been hers. The bed was parallel to a tall window, which had a view of the mansion's gardens. She climbed into it, not caring about the dust on the sheets. Or about the bird droppings by the window. Or about falling asleep in her clothes.

❦

Liam touched his fingers to the walls of the first floor and tapped lightly. He thought he was lucky to have met Angela. He genuinely liked her. He'd had many friends, but no one seemed to get him like she did. He wished she would get her memories back quickly; if anyone could crack the case, it was her. He needed her back on the story of Jack Roe as soon as possible.

He tapped lightly (and diligently) on the walls of each room, the kitchen, library, study, and servant quarters with no luck. Just the non-echo of his absorbed taps. However, the living room wall gave feedback in several places, which meant that those spaces were hollow. Liam stopped. *The cellar must be behind this wall. Someone must have sealed it.*

But there was nothing he could do at that moment. He needed an ax or hammer to break it down. He almost couldn't wait to tell Angela the next morning.

❦

Angela stretched her arms and legs. She looked out the window. Although the garden was overgrown, it was stunning. It featured a large number of roses. They were tall and untrimmed, as were the trees and bushes. The birds chirped away in their garden paradise. She couldn't imagine why she'd ever wanted to move to the city. To leave her mother and this beautiful place.

Her name was Angela Wise, and she was staring out a window, wondering who she was, and how she got there. She was ready to look for more information again and hoped that she and Liam would have more success than the previous day.

She smiled, thinking of her only friend. She didn't know much, but she felt like she knew him.

She looked in the closet and found comfortable looking sweatpants and a t-shirt. She lucked out; they fit. She raised her hair in a messy bun. When she went down the spiral staircase Liam was already standing at the bottom with two coffee cups.

"Good morning, Angela." Liam seemed a little too happy. He handed her a cup of steaming coffee. "Got these at Mr. Al's Supermarket a few blocks down. Nice guy."

"That was nice of you. You seem pretty chipper today."

"I have good news; I'm almost sure I found the cellar." Liam quickly turned and began walking.

Angela knew he was leading the way for her without asking, but she was happy to follow as they entered the family room.

He pointed straight at the wall. "It's right here."

"I see a white wall. Am I looking at it wrong?"

"It's behind this wall. I wonder why anyone would seal this thing. Anyway, there's something here." He gave it a hard knock and put his ear to the wall. "Hear that?"

She leaned her head forward. "Hear what?"

"It's hollow, which means there is something there."

"How do we get in?"

"We're going to have to break it."

"And how long will that take?" Angela felt like she should be aghast, shocked that someone would mention puncturing the walls in her home. But the home wasn't really hers. And it was just a wall. Liam seemed so excited. If he was willing to bust through the wall, she figured it would be for a good reason, given his reluctance to ruin anything with value.

"About an hour, maybe a little more. Depends on how fast we hammer through this."

Angela looked at the clock above the fireplace. It was broken. "What time is it?"

Liam peeked at his watch. "Ten."

"I have to get down to the studio soon, but I suppose I could be a little late." She couldn't resist the mystery of what was behind the wall. Plus, this sounded much more fun than working.

Liam clapped his hands. "Let's do this!"

She liked it when he was himself, not hiding who he was around her as he did around others. Real Liam was the Liam she felt connected to, the one who had nothing to fear or hide. She sensed that he felt handcuffed. Society pushed him into an uncomfortable corner where he had to pretend to be somebody he wasn't.

"I'm going to look for a hammer in the garage," he said, then sped off.

The house phone rang, and since Angela didn't know what else to do, she answered it. It was the studio. They wanted her to cover for John again. It seemed to her that John was a lazy piece of pie. Thankfully, she caught herself up on the news station and the employees working there. John was the face of mid-morning news. From what she learned, they read off the prepared script, so covering for him wouldn't be a problem in that sense. She knew she couldn't ditch the station now.

Liam returned ten minutes later, clearly proud of himself for finding the hammer, as he held it like some trophy. "Ready?"

She sighed. "No."

He dropped the hand that held the hammer to his side. "Why? What happened?"

"Studio's been looking for me. Apparently, they rang the apartment over and over until they found this number. They want me there in an hour."

"I understand." He lowered his eyes to the hammer, that childlike pride shifted to deflation.

"We both know how important it is for me to go to the studio. We're just going to have to leave this for a later time. Let's come back tonight."

"Deal."

Angela ran upstairs to change. In a matter of minutes, they were in the car, driving back to the city.

"You sure you'll be ok alone in there?" Liam asked as they stood in front of the studio gates.

"I'm sure. Besides, I won't be alone. I've got that Robert guy." She laughed.

"If you need anything, call me." He handed her his business card which read: *Take a peek at Liam's Antique.*

THE DEAL

JULIA
Winter
Late 1930s

Dark witches will hunt you down in an otherwise normal world. Please be careful. You were likely left in the dark about all of this, and if I do one thing right in my life it is this: I will not allow you to suffer the fate that I did.

—A LETTER

Day turned into night. Julia curled up in a circle, hugging her knees. She shivered, but she was tired enough to drift into a deep sleep.

Julia awoke to something jabbing her upper back.

"Ed? It's about time," she said, rubbing her back. Before she could get up and face him, she felt another sharp poke. "Ouch!" she screamed.

"Get up, girl." The demanding voice did not belong to Ed.

Julia quickly studied the form in front of her. The woman was about three feet tall and looked ancient. Julia turned away initially. She took a deep breath before looking back to the misshapen thing that was addressing her.

The woman had a hunched back, and her compact legs limped as she closed the space between herself and Julia. Her neck was almost non-existent. Something above the bridge of her nose was pulsating. She held a sharp-ended cane, which must have supported the weight of her left side, as her legs clearly could not do such a thing. Julia felt the blood drain from her face and the pallid color it left behind. She got up and backed away prepared to run to the station's exit. She didn't want to be near that creature.

The strange woman barked out an order. "Come on girl, follow me. I have something to show you." She extended her long, bony finger. "Don't be afraid, I'm here to help you." Julia noticed that just one chipped tooth peeked out from her mouth as the woman tried to smile, but miserably failed. Her head, with the few hairs that remained atop it, resembled a strange coconut. Her eyes were drooping, heavy, and clouded with little life in them.

Julia took her eyes off the exit sign "Help me? Please find somewhere else to spread your nonsense. You can't help me."

The woman smirked. "Yes, Julia. I can." Although she looked frail, her voice was sharp and commanding.

Julia felt her face twist into the contortion of confusion. After years of perfecting the art of steeling herself, her knees shook. "How do know my name?"

"Follow me and you shall know." Her intruder limped into the night. Julia followed hesitantly. Although she was terrified of the thing in front of her, she followed, as though some great force *commanded* her to do so.

The New York blocks stood miraculously empty, and the night seemed darker than Julia imagined possible. As they turned onto murky alleys and crossed countless vacant blocks, the holes in Julia's shoes welcomed an influx of freezing snow onto her bare toes. Julia stopped, as her ice-covered feet no longer felt the earth beneath her. But the strange woman persisted, promising Julia warmth, repeating the same things. "Don't be frightened, you shall warm up soon enough. Follow me."

The duo reached a building smacked right in the middle of a prominent neighborhood which lacked street signs. She knew the streets of the city well, in the library she read history books and looked at pictures of old structures. But she'd never seen a building like this. It looked more ancient than the bizarre woman who dragged Julia into the dead night. What was more bizarre was the height of the building. It housed seven floors, which—according to the history encyclopedia she picked up a few weeks ago—were too many stories for such an old structure.

"Follow, follow. I promise you answers." The limping woman waved for Julia to walk through the damaged front door.

"I came this far because you promised warmth," Julia said, stopping about twelve feet behind the woman. "And this dump here, this don't look like warmth." She pointed at the broken windows and missing doors. "I'm not following you any farther, for all I know you're off your rocker."

"Is that so? Don't you want answers?"

Julia kept her arms at her sides, thought she wanted to cross them. Wanted that useless gesture of protection. "Answers to what?"

"How I know your name, for one?"

Julia looked at her shoes. Her feet felt heavy and frozen—numb She was mad. Mad at the strange woman, and mad at herself for being reckless enough to follow her.

"You could have heard my name at the train station when I was speaking with Ed. So right now, I don't give a damn how you know it. Hell, I don't give a damn why you dragged me out here. I'm freezing, I lost my spot at the station, missed out on food, and I forgot my cup. So, you can go into that miscarriage of a building alone." Shame and guilt mingled in Julia's gut. Life on the streets had taught her that none of this was intelligent. That she should run. But her feet were frozen in more than one way.

"Follow me upstairs and you shall get warmth, I promise you."

"I may be a street beggar, but I'm not stupid, and you have no right to kid with me. I have changed my mind. I'm not following you, you old ugly hag."

"Oh, but I think you will," the woman replied with a crooked smile. She reached into her coat and pulled out a silver heart locket dangling from a delicate chain. It showcased an engraved pattern of roses, intertwined with a vine that almost camouflaged the initial J.

"Where did you get that?" Julia whispered. The locket was hers. Julia's parents had gifted it to her on her seventh birthday. She desperately wanted it back. It had her parents' pictures inside. She wanted to see their smiles again. And the message. There was a message written behind her mother's photograph: *pure love breaks evil.*

"I see you have more questions. As I have mentioned, I have the answers. Come with me," the woman said. She then tucked the locket back into her coat and wobbled toward the building.

Julia was close enough to the woman that she could pick her pocket and claim what was rightfully hers.

"Don't try it. No one steals from me," the woman hissed.

"I think you have it the other way around, twit. That locket belongs to me." The old lady just laughed and continued forward.

Julia had no choice. She lifted her heavy feet and followed the precious locket. The steps she took pained her so much. Much more than when she walked barefoot through the streets. Before she'd found shoes. At least then, she'd had callouses to protect her.

Inside, Julia smelled rust and mold. Light from the full yellow moon above seeped into the building through the windows that faced it. She heard rats parading around the enclosed area. From the darkness, as her eyes continued to adjust, a large staircase with missing pieces of cracked wood materialized before her. She pinched her nostrils to protect them from the stench of the old woman—it was like rotten potatoes.

"I said, give me what belongs to me."

"Oh, stop with your yap, child. I shall give it to you, just follow me."

"How did you get your hands on it?"

"Come, I shall explain all."

"Not, until you give me that locket."

"Suit yourself."

The woman picked up a dusty lantern and a matchbook, against which she struck a match to stick in the glass. The light of the lantern, dimmed by years of dust, was strong enough to expose the rest of the staircase. The woman took baby steps up the stairs, which scared the scurrying rat residents of the building, breaking the eerie silence. Julia clenched her fists. Annoyed, she followed the old woman and stopped several times to allow her to catch her breath.

Then something happened that Julia imagined she'd hallucinated. The earth opened up and swallowed them down into its core. Like they were nothing. The darkness was so thick and prevalent it drew them downward in the same manner a helium balloon would float upward. Effortlessly. Her new surroundings were so dark. Julia felt as though her eyes might never adjust. She heard the flow of a river. When her eyes did adjust, she saw that the river flowed red. A coppery odor, like an old penny, swirled around her. That was a blood river. There was no water. The rocky hills and mountains behind her emitted booming sounds that she imagined would accompany an explosion.

The woman lost her limp, and Julia thought she saw, just above the bridge of the woman's nose, something moving, like the sound of a single heartbeat sound in visual form. When it stopped pulsing, a slit opened, exposing an additional eye. Julia sprang back.

"Where the hell are we?" She demanded. And who—or *what*—the hell are you?"

"We are... in what you humans call hell." The woman answered as though this were an every-day place that every-day people knew. A regular occurrence. As though it was a non-issue.

It was an issue. "Get me outta here, get me outta here! I can't breathe!" Julia yelled.

"Oh, don't be dramatic. You are an Ortor. I do not need your histrionics. Ortors can breathe and see here."

Julia coughed, the air nearly fleeing her lungs. But when she inhaled again, there was no pain. "Ortor? What? You know what—I no. I do not care. I said get me outta here or—"

"Or what?" The woman continued to walk down the narrow, bumpy walkway that followed the flow of the blood river. The destination appeared to be a dark forest. The trees glistened silver in spots. Metal. Leaves as though they were hand-forged and polished to a sleek shine clinked against one another. The woman's yellow eye acted as a candle; projecting enough light for Julia to see what was before them.

"Or I die here. I'm not taking another step forward." Julia intermittently felt like she was struggling to catch her breath, but she managed to speak.

"Oh, boogers. You can be so annoying. It is just much, much easier down here. But as you wish."

Within a minute they were back in the run-down building. Somehow, they rose, not climbed, to the seventh floor. Julia took a deep breath. It smelled like her world again. She saw darkness through the missing doors. But a door labeled 77 to the right remained intact.

The woman placed her lantern that shook, along with her hands, on the floor. Then, she pulled out an ancient looking skeleton key to open the door.

A thousand candles greeted them upon entry. Warmth finally crept into Julia's shoes, and her toes tingled as the numbness dissipated. The woman walked over to a worn-down futon. Julia noticed more furniture, all full of holes. A wooden chair sat with a small, dusty, and rectangular table. A large translucent sphere and a deck of cards were nestled in the center of a dozen candles atop the table.

Julia closed her eyes for a moment, happily taking in the heat. Warmth had often helped her forget her burdens—maybe it would help her forget hell.

"I can free you of your burden, child," the woman interrupted Julia's moment of joy, limping to the table. "I desire to help you. That is all."

Julia walked to the couch and sunk into the hollow cushions. She was afraid but she also felt that she had nothing left to lose. She rubbed her legs.

"Who the hell are you?"

"Haven't' you figured it out?" The woman laughed. "It's clear as night and day, isn't it?"

"Night is not so clear. If it is 'clear as day,' I must be in the dark. What is?"

"I'm not human. Silly girl. I'm a witch."

"Witches don't exist, you crazy hag." Julia ignored the retreating of the third eye. She pretended it was an every-day thing, that every-day people had seen. This was how she coped with the extraordinary at that moment.

The woman lifted a knotted finger and waved it at Julia. "Read too much non-fiction in that library of yours, I see." She walked over to the table and wrapped her hands around the deck of cards. "Fiction is where truth lives, in many forms, but let us move on. We exist. Witches. There are more of us than you can imagine. Hasn't our journey proved anything to you?"

Julia ignored the question. "What do you want from me? I just want an explanation for that locket you have."

The woman's eyes sparked with anger. "Not just yet."

"You got some nerve, grandma. You owe me an explanation."

"Let us say I had a deal, if you will, with your parents. That is how I got the locket. But for now... tell me, child, about that handsome red-haired fella."

"What do you know about my parents?" Julia exclaimed, jumping to her feet, ignoring the question about her crush.

The witch just laughed.

"I knew it. You are one crazy twit." Julia ran to the door.

"Do you not want the locket?" Ignoring Julia's outburst, the woman replied. "I can also help you win *him*."

"I'm done with your game." Julia closed her hand into a fist, ready to punch the woman. She hesitated. She had never attached anybody before. Especially an elderly person. But this woman was not as frail as she appeared. As Julia prepared to take a swipe at the woman, she saw the locket dangling from *his* fingers. He wore the same long coat as he had that morning. He carried the same smile, and his eyes investigated hers. Like he was inside them, like he knew everything about the world. Even its creation.

Julia unclenched her fists and took a few steps closer. She was so close to him now; she smelled his cologne. She saw the blue wash over the little green in his eyes. Her heart almost jumped out of her chest.

"We can be together, and you can have this," he said, dangling the chain with the locket in front of her. His was voice deep, and his smile was wide.

"We can? I can?" She was answering, but it was as though she was doing so while asleep. She knew what she was saying and why she was saying it, but she didn't know how it was all happening. It was like she was being controlled, but at the same time, like she had the freedom to say what she wanted.

"But of course." The words flowed from his mouth.

"How?" she asked.

"Just tell me. Tell me now. Do you want to be with me at any cost?"

"Yes. I want to be with you. At any cost." Now she felt dispatched from herself. She was answering in a trance. Her mind was in a fog. Was she in her own head, or was someone else pulling the strings?

"Perfect." He opened his mouth to speak, but the screechy sound of the old woman replaced his deep voice. His daring blue eyes turned into lifeless yellow pinholes, and his smooth skin scrunched into a thousand wrinkles.

Julia gasped at the vision of the old woman, standing just where Jack had been, and the old woman spoke: "I will take your firstborn child as payment."

"What?" Julia demanded. "Like hell you will. I would never let that happen."

"You're right about that, but it matters not," the old woman laughed gleefully through her words. "Let me explain. The darling man you so adore has a wife and children, and how torturous that will be for you. Well, you asked to be with him, and I will make that happen for you, but as we both mentioned and acknowledged, it will come at a cost, of course."

Julia's throat made an animal noise. Like a growl. "You crazy woman."

"Not so crazy, you see. I already told you I am a witch. I do not understand why that is so difficult for you to believe, even after I took you down below. You still refuse to see the truth. Refuse to see what is in front of you. Your parents and I had a deal, but they did not hold up their end of the bargain. So now I must make a deal with you, and *you* will pay off their debt."

Julia's vision swirled and her mind raced. "What deal?"

"The deal we just made, silly. You said you wanted to be with him at any cost. Well, I have just told you that cost, you disgusting Ortor filth. Your firstborn will belong to me."

"I'm filth? You're the one who tricked me into making what you're calling a *deal* with you! I did no such thing! I was talking with Jack, and in no way did I offer you my firstborn child!" Julia's face heated, flushed with rage.

"Oh dear, it is not my fault that you could not see what was right before you. Poor thing. Tsk. That will be your downfall. What do you humans say? Oh! Yes! The apple falls not far from the tree, correct? Your parents had similar issues with their vision. Perhaps you should get that checked."

"What do you know about my parents? And give me that locket." Julia was so angry her fingers once again curled into fists. She hoped to land a punch on the old woman's distorted face. Distort it further.

The woman ignored Julia's questions. Instead, she placed her hands on one of the burning candles. She closed her droopy eyes, which pointed at the mirror across the table, and chanted something Julia couldn't understand.

"Tell me now, you crazy twit. So help me, I will bust your face up so bad your ugly eyes will fall out of their sockets. You'll be more attractive for it, too. I will break your little crooked legs and you will limp no more."

"You shall find your parents' path soon enough, just not tonight," she replied.

Julia wished to pounce on the old thing, but the woman's blood-curdling gaze stopped her from moving anywhere.

As if she'd won a prize, the witch said, "It's done. He will fall in love with you. But remember, Julia, our deal, the Ortor—your child—will belong to me." She smiled slyly.

An inhumane laugh hugged the room. The candles burned until the drapes, table, couch, and all the contents in the apartment vanished in an aggressive smoke. Julia looked around for the woman, but she disappeared, leaving only a screechy echo behind:

"We shall meet again."

The flames closed in on her. There was nowhere to run. Her lungs filled with smoke. She grew dizzy and coughed as she tried to gasp for air, but the air felt stiff. Un-inhalable. She choked, her eyes filled with tears from the smoke, and her skin burned to a point where she felt excruciating pain. As her eyes closed, her brain sent the message to her lungs that there was no clean air to breathe. Julia felt the hard floor beneath her sluggish frame, and all went blank.

FLEETING MEMORIES

ANGELA
Fall
Early 1970s

My mother—your grandmother—nearly saved me from the clutches of a dark witch... Because my mother could not fully save me, I was doomed to a life of begging on the streets without knowledge of most of my past life. Typically, dark witches are easy to detect. You would know not to follow such a witch simply because they offer you lavish things, or what your heart most desires. I did not know this. I was innocent, young, and homeless.

— A LETTER

The fallen leaves painted a beautiful picture on the sidewalk. All the greens, reds, and yellows. Angela loved to crunch the dry leaves with her feet. She wondered if that was something she liked to do as a child. She wondered if fall was her favorite season. This made sense to her. Autumn was full of lively colors, then almost instantly, it shed its external beauty, laying those beautiful dead leaves out for people to step on, leaving the trees empty. Autumn was unafraid of its nakedness. Forgetting about its past, how lively it was, before it all stripped away into a pool of crunchy mush on the ground.

Some of the fallen leaves landed on her windowsill. It had been a month, and Angela had only gotten sparks of memories here and there, but she couldn't recall enough to put the puzzle of her life back together. She remembered a beautiful blonde woman, parading around the house in a green silk gown. The woman wore slippers with small heels, and she barked orders at Angela. She also remembered how the woman yelled. Practicing spells, spells, and more spells. Angela just couldn't understand what that meant, she guessed that woman was Zilda—her mother—as Edward had said. The yelling to practice spells seemed strange. The only thing Angela could relate spells to was fairytales. She speculated that maybe her mother had suffered a mental illness.

She looked at the London Plane Tree across the street from her apartment window. It had almost entirely changed its colors. She thought of Liam and how much she missed him. She couldn't believe that the last time she saw him was a month ago. Just before she left the car as he dropped her off at the studio. He phoned her that same day and said he had to tend to some unexpected work in France, and that he was leaving.

It was that time of the day. Five o'clock on a Wednesday, their usual time to catch up. She couldn't wait to hear Liam on the other line. He was to return the following week.

When the call did come, the words on the other end were not reassuring; "I'm not returning this week, either."

"I wish you would come back, Liam. It's so lonely here."

"I know. I'm so sorry. I promise it won't be long. One more week. They want me to walk over a few chateaus. And I can't quit on them now. I don't get clients from France too often. I gotta tell you, France is a beauty."

"But I need you here," Angela replied. She recognized that she sounded like a stubborn child.

"Have you had a chance to break that wall down yet?" he asked. She heard him hold his breath on the other line.

"I'm not doing it without you, Liam, you know that."

Liam sighed. "Give it one more week, and we'll get to it together. One more week. Tell me how you are?"

"I'm better, trying to hang on to the last case I was working on. I had expected the case, and work to help me remember more. I've tried to spend more time at the studio. Robert's picked up on my memory loss. He started to ask me things I couldn't answer. He knows I had memory loss. I suppose the others realized I've been acting strangely. I had to tell them what happened. My doctor sent them a note. They let me take time off, as much as I needed. They've kept me on the case, even. I mean, it seems like this case is what keeps the folks at the studio on edge. And to tell you the truth, I like working on it. It keeps my mind occupied."

"I'm glad they're respecting your needs, Angela. And that you still get to work on the Roe case." Liam said.

"Me too. I read my research. I'm putting the pieces together... again, I suppose. I also found more leads. I just have to visit his family to interview. I'll tell you all about it when you get back."

"No. Don't visit his family. Not yet, I mean. Let's wait until you get some memories back? Maybe? You don't want to overwhelm yourself. I'll help you with it as soon as I land in New York," he said.

Angela sighed. "Maybe you're right. I'll just try to visit the mansion to see if I can trigger any more memories." She shrugged. I saw the doctor. He told me I'm improving immensely, and it's possible that I'll be back to normal soon. He said something like this 'it will hit you out of nowhere when you least expect it.'"

"I'm glad to hear you are remembering. I can't wait to see your face." There was some background noise, men talking. "So sorry, but duty calls. I have to go now. See you in a week."

After they said their goodbyes, Angela decided to visit the mansion. She called for a cab. As nervous as she was, she managed to fall asleep on the way. When she awoke, she recognized the empty streets of Long Island. Just ten minutes and she was there. When she walked up to the double doors, a picture from a movie-like reality she had seen upon her last visit flashed in her mind. She saw the woman again—her mother. She was beautiful, and she was standing at the entryway, her lips tight. She called Angela inside the house, talking about spells, and magic, and worlds below. These were familiar things. Spells and magic, and Angela felt as though she had believed in them. But she didn't now.

She remembered going to the kitchen, looking through jars of odd things, snakes, spiders, a collection of random animal eyes, and some herbs and spices. She remembered telling her mother that she didn't want anything to do with magic. She wanted a normal life.

"Beware of what you say, child," her mother would answer, rubbing the bridge of her nose. "You are lucky to live, to learn the trade. Filthy Ortors." And that's all she could retrieve from her mind that day. The flashes became more frequent, but not enough to put all the pieces together.

She hated when her memories worked against her. Magic was not real, and she questioned why it was lurking inside her head. Why it felt so real. It was impossible. She blamed the amnesia, the accident, anything but reality. Because it could not be.

INTRODUCTIONS

ANGELA

I was so foolish. I hope you'll forgive me for the words I will write next.

What I wanted, more than anything, was a life with your father... Your father belonged to me. But his love—it was not real. That love was produced by a spell. Child, at first, I did not mind. That's the biggest sin I must confess. Though you may find my confessions afterward to be dreadful, still, they hold no candle to the original sin, which was acceptance of an unrequited love. That unrequited love was all I had.

— A LETTER

It was early morning, and although a chill was in the air, the sun peeked out for Angela to allow the warmth of its light to seep into her being. She impatiently looked at the time.

One more minute and Liam would land.

She walked into the airport, looking for the tall figure wearing his signature grey coat.

"Liam," she shouted as soon as she spotted him in a large crowd of travelers.

"Angela!" He waved back and ran to her. She eased into his open arms for a bear hug. Not wasting a minute, they began to chat.

"What happened to your hair?" She picked up a small brown curl from underneath his hat.

"You just haven't seen me in while. It's done what hair likes to do—it's grown."

"It looks like an unruly mop," she joked.

"I'm so glad you like it. And gladder to be back. You won't believe the news I recently got from my mother."

"Do tell."

They started toward the exit.

Liam stopped and turned to her. "I'm sorry. How are you doing? I must know that before anything else!"

"I'm ok, doing the same old memory loss remedies, you know." She smiled. "I'm getting some of them back, piece by piece. But nothing that makes sense or to help put it all together yet."

"Sounds better than it was when I left. That's great. Maybe everything will be back soon." He placed his hand on hers and gave her a warm smile. "One good thing that came out of the horrid situation with your memory loss and that piece of trash that kidnapped you is that we met each other."

"I'm glad I met you, too, Liam." She stopped to give him another hug. When they started walking again, she asked, "So, what's the news?"

"My little sister is getting married. And they're having an engagement party. Today. Can you believe it? Today. And I'm going, even with the jet lag."

"Oh wow, congratulations. That's amazing news!" Angela said. She hailed a cab and jumped in with Liam, after he placed his one piece of luggage in the trunk.

"Where to?" The driver asked.

"Midtown," Liam said.

"Midtown? Are you not going home first?"

"The party starts at six, so we have to hurry. We can go to Midtown first so you can get ready."

"We? Ready?"

Liam stopped for a moment and looked at his watch.

"Yes. It's only 3:10. I know how you girls are with getting ready. So, you'll have plenty of time."

Angela huffed. "I'm not that bad. Well, ok. Maybe a little." She smiled and nudged him. "You want me to attend as your guest?"

"Of course. I want you to meet my family. I mean, I've been raving about you to them for the past few months. They cannot wait to meet you. And I want *you* to celebrate this marvelous occasion with my family."

"I guess I could use a break." She took a breath. "How was your trip?"

"Loved it. I got to tour some of the chateaus. One of them was an interesting find. The chateau of MonBlanc. It's marvelously beautiful, even in its abandoned state. According to the French, it was home to powerful beings who were at constant war with witches. The witches are rumored to have won as the powerful beings died out. The witches had one rule. They couldn't fall in love, or they would be forced back to hell. One witch disobeyed her master, fell in love. Her master couldn't kill her, but he did remove a piece of her heart and froze it into a red ruby. He then banned her to the forest of the damned, in a world below our own. Legend says the ruby is a good luck charm to anyone who wears it."

Angela, who loved good stories, enjoyed Liam's tale. Though it was a bit dark. "Fun Legend."

Liam dug in his pocket and removed something. "This is for you."

Angela gave her friend a warm smile as she took a box from his extended hand and opened it. Inside was a bracelet that showcased a red ruby.

"Funny story. They sell these around the chateau for tourists. I bought it at the gift shop. Then went to a jewelry store to get my sister a wedding gift and saw this incredible ruby staring at me. Switched the fake one out with this. Thought you would love it."

Angela was struck by his thoughtfulness, and for a moment, she couldn't speak. How kind of him it was to have done that for her! "Liam, thank you! I-I don't know how I usually respond to such nice things. It's lovely. Thank you." She put it on her wrist right away. "I'm never taking this off." As excited and touched as she was, a little pull in the back of her mind was calling to her. It was a feeling, associated with the witches, and the bracelet. She shook her head, as though the motion would shake the thoughts from her mind. A small dreadful feeling remained. Faint, but there.

Back at her apartment, Angela dressed herself in an exquisite silver and blue dress. Its modest sequins sparkled, complimenting her deep green-blue eyes. Her curves were accentuated in all the right places. She slipped on short heels to add a little height. Her red hair was peeking shyly from a royal blue hat. She thought she was a pretty enough woman and didn't want much make-up, so she applied a faint amount of blush and a light pink lipstick. She finished with a dab of silver eyeshadow and some mascara. She grabbed her white gloves and purse.

"You're glowing. Gorgeous, Stunning. Wow," Liam exclaimed as he met her downstairs by his car. His face was alight, and Angela was pleased by this reaction. It was genuine coming from him.

They arrived at a large white house in the south of Long Island. The sun had sunk, and a full, yellow moon replaced it. Decorative lights glowed in the distance. Angela could hear music and distinct voices coming from the house.

After they knocked on the door, a short, attractive woman opened it and welcomed Liam with a long embrace.

"Liam dear!"

"Ma, meet Angela. Angela Wise. My newest and dearest friend."

His mother smiled brightly and reached for Angela's hand. "Very nice to meet you, we've heard so much about you. Oh, and of course we see you on the news all the time. I *loved* the latest report you did on the college campus scandal. And the one—"

"Ma," Liam interrupted.

"Ok, ok, I'll stop. Now come with me."

She led them to the backyard. The grassy area was warm. An outdoor fireplace illuminated the area, lending a soft glow and heat to the chilly night. A bar was situated next to a gigantic pool. The water was crystal blue, illuminated by pool lights. Waiters walked from the bar to the guests, all with the same stance: one white-gloved hand behind their backs and another below the trays they carried. She heard their suggestions of wine and hors d'oeuvres.

"Come, I want you to meet my sister Layla." Liam broke her investigation of the scene, dragging her off.

Layla had deep blue eyes and red hair that resembled Angela's. She wore an ivory gown. She smiled as she showed the guests her engagement ring. The man Liam pointed out as Layla's fiancé chatted with other guests off in the distance, but his puppy eyes were locked on Layla. Angela wondered if she had ever loved someone.

Once Liam got Layla's attention, he introduced Angela.

Layla beamed at her. "Oh, Ms. Wise! This is such a pleasure. I, like so many, am quite a fan."

"Formalities later ladies," Liam said, giving his sister a twirl to admire her dress. He hugged her tightly. "I can't believe that you, out of three of us, and the youngest one may I add, are the first one to get hitched." His eyes trailed off to the other end of the yard. "Speaking of the three of us, where is Caiden?"

"He's around here somewhere." Layla swiveled her head a bit until she locked in on her target. She pointed to indicate where Caiden was. "Oh. Right there by the pool. He's with Jim, my fiancé, come let me introduce you." Layla smiled, leading the way.

Liam tapped Angela's shoulder. "I have to tell you something. I've been meaning to tell you for a while, but. Anyway, it's time you know."

Angela's stomach knotted. Was it bad? Were her instincts as immemorable as her life? "Now? Ok," she said.

"Since you're here, it will be a bit easier, plus it will help both of us in..."

Before Liam could finish his sentence, Layla turned around. "Liam meet Jim. Jim, this is my other brother Liam."

Angela dwelled on how she wished to remember her own family, her mother. Not just vague snippets of them. She felt a hint of nervousness. Had she always been nervous when meeting new people? She looked to the bracelet. Maybe it was the blonde woman from her memories that upset her... she shook her head again and tuned in to the conversation.

"Jim, a pleasure. You best take care of my little sis, or else Caiden and I will have to bury you somewhere," he said jocularly, but with a glint of warning in his eyes. Angela hadn't seen that side of Liam.

"Enough, Liam. He's just being a big brother, Jim. Don't mind him."

Liam gestured to another man Angela didn't recognize. He walked over with a big smile. He turned the man's attention to Angela.

"While we're at introductions, Caiden this is Angela, a very good friend of mine. Angela, this is Caiden, our oldest brother."

"Very nice to meet you," Caiden said in a smooth voice, taking Angela's hand to kiss it. When they touched, something jarred inside her, and she liked it. Her knees buckled, if she were any closer to the pool, she'd have been at risk of falling in.

His deep brown eyes projected a great kindness, and quite a bit of class. His smile was brilliant. Fission and goosebumps crept up her body. The feeling rose to her cheeks, and it warmed them to what she knew was a hot red color. She pretended to hold on to Liam as a means of showing affection, but she was using him as a prop to keep her balance.

She returned Caiden's smile, hoping he wouldn't notice her blush. She knew she had to get away from him as soon as possible, unless she wanted everyone to watch her trip over nothing but her own feet and a strange feeling. She cursed her knees for betraying her. Without a word she half-stumbled, half-ran to the bar. Caiden must have followed her, and quickly because just after she took her seat, she watched him move with the grace of a leopard as he slid to sit next to her. How smooth each movement was.

"So how did you and Liam meet?" he asked after he sat.

Angela cleared her throat. "It's a long story" she managed, trying not to look at him.

"I like long stories." He smiled. "Especially from someone as stunning as you."

Angela blushed again, and her stomach flipped. *Compose yourself. He's only a man. A very handsome one, but still, only a man,* she told herself.

"We, um, we met in the city, after my accident. Liam saved me, and we've been great friends since."

"Accident?" Caiden asked, then shifted his eyes to Liam, who followed them to the bar. "You saved her? You're going around saving women and not telling anyone about it?"

Liam continued to smile. "Right place right time, I guess."

Caiden stared at his brother. "So that's... that's all you are planning to say about that, I suppose." He looked back at Angela and inclined his head. "Please, go on."

"Yeah. I was hit by a car, and then..." she trailed off for a moment, wondering if this man would even believe her. Why hadn't Liam said anything about her yet? She chuckled and shrugged. "Well, then I was kidnapped by this crazy man, who happened to be your brother's neighbor. And your brother saved me. He's been so helpful since. I owe him my life."

She took a small gulp of wine from her glass. She hoped to change the subject but ended up telling him something stupid without intention. The words just fell out of her mouth, it seemed. "Liam hasn't talked about you much." She bit her lip and took another sip. *Why would I even tell him that?*

"Is that so?" He laughed. Caiden didn't look offended. He brushed his long fingers over his dark hair. Angela noticed his crescent-moon eyebrows were thick and dark. His angular cheekbones carved down towards a stubborn jaw, and she loved it.

"Can't blame him. I haven't been around much. My life revolves around business trips and work."

"I guess you two have something in common, then," Angela said.

Liam slapped Caiden's shoulder. "Just enough that we've yet to become estranged," Liam said.

"It must be exciting to travel so much," she said. Though she wanted to change the subject. Talking about Caiden only fed into her odd and instant admiration. The way his mouth moved, the way his voice vibrated, and his smell. It reminded her of oranges and summer.

"It is. For now. I took after my father's real estate and jewelry lines. I enjoy the business world very much. But sooner rather than later I want to settle down, with the right girl." His brown eyes flashed.

Angela wanted to sit with Caiden forever, but it seemed too fast, too unreal. She needed a distraction. Didn't Liam want to tell her something important? She turned to face him, but he was no longer next to them.

When she returned to her drink, she caught a glimpse of Caiden. This time Angela felt a wave of pleasant electricity. This situation seemed too good to be true. The chemistry was undeniable. They sat talking for hours from the short distance they held between them on the bar stools. It felt as though she was in his arms. The warmth was surreal. Wild. Angela liked it, but at the same time, she hated that she felt like she was losing control.

She noticed how Caiden couldn't help but look at her. His eyes spoke volumes.

She sipped from her glass, telling herself it would be un-ladylike to confess that she already had the hots for him. She couldn't make the first move or be pushy. She was sure he had girls lined up for him. Why would he want her?

LONG-AWAITED ENCOUNTER

JULIA
Winter
Late 1930s

Your father, however, had another family. It was as though that part of his life was a blank spot. Though he would go missing for several days, I thought nothing of it, as his work called him often to travel. That was my second sin—not questioning my life. Of course, there would be terrible repercussions to the spell I so happily accepted.

— A LETTER

The city noise shook Julia awake. She opened her eyes, reading the sign in front of her: *42nd and BROADWAY*.

It was still early morning, but the cold was bearable Her throat ached from the fumes of the night before. She tried to shake the encounter from her mind. She looked forward to the one thing that made her happy. His face. His big bright smile. His sweet "Good morning."

She found a dirty cup on the sidewalk, ready to face another day of begging. She hugged her knees to her chest while she waited for someone—anyone—to show her mercy. Sure, she was hoping for a specific someone, but she was desperate. Anyone would do. It was another ordinary day, void of compassion from the more fortunate. If only he passed by her, she was sure he would spare change. Her stomach was empty, and her throat was dry.

"Hey, you," his warm voice penetrated her heart. There was a different gleam in his eyes; it wasn't just the usual kindness he offered; it was *more*. He had never greeted her in such a casual manner.

"Look at you. You must be freezing. You need a warm bath, some food, and warm clothes. You should not be out in the elements as you are."

Is he talking to me? Is he offering me help? Julia looked around to make sure there was no one else. *It's a dream, definitely a dream.* Her mouth dropped open, and she stared at his gorgeous face.

"Well? Come on now. Don't just stare at me with those eyes." He gently tugged on her arm, helping her to her feet. He gripped her hand and pulled her closer to him, urging her to follow. The pleasant scent of his fresh cologne hit her nostrils.

"My name is Jack. Jack Roe. And you are?"

"Juh-Julia," she managed in a quiet stutter.

"Julia," he repeated, his voice like a dream. "I have to run to work, but I will situate you in my apartment. It's not too far from here. You can clean yourself up, eat something, and get new clothes."

"Why are you helping me?" she asked. She wanted to believe that he was kind and generous, but her experiences had jaded her. Was she wrong to feel suspicious of him? So many people kicked and belittled her. No one showed her respect, or even regarded her as a human. At times she felt an invisible burden. Who would want to help her? After taking another look at him and a look at the cold corner that was her home, she decided she had nothing to lose. She wanted to hold on to *hope*. Hope. It was such an impossible thing to conjure. It had been for most of her life. But she felt it stir somewhere.

His eyes sparkled like blue diamonds extracted from the holiest places on earth. "This morning I saw something in you. I don't quite know how to explain it. You—without speaking—pulled me to you. You need help And I can help you, so why shouldn't I? Why hasn't anyone else? It simply makes no sense."

Everything happened so fast. Her legs felt like they couldn't hold the weight of her body. A vast number of things could have made her feel this frail. Her hunger often weakened her and so did the cold. She wondered if Jack was somehow weakening her as well. His offer had stunned her. Her heart thundered, and she tried to speak, but anxiety or shock held her voice captive. Luckily, she didn't have to say a word; he did all the talking.

Manhattan's streets were filled with people who were in a hurry to reach their destinations. Jack, who was still holding her hand to make sure she did not fall behind, was no exception. He walked with a brisk stride, and Julia skipped to keep up with him. She didn't notice the cold now, her legs regained their strength, she was ready to follow Jack to the lowest depths of hell if she had to.

"Here we are." He stopped in front of a building. Inside the elevator, Julia was able to focus on him. He was perfect. He even shone in a way. His auburn curls put a smile on her face. She was inside an elevator for crying out loud. With a guy she could have (and often had) only dreamed about, and he was so close she heard his breathing. And to top that off—by the looks of the building he took her through—it appeared as though he was filthy rich. The unreality of it all had her heart skipping a few beats. She watched as he opened his leather brief-case and pulled out a set of keys.

The jaw-dropping beauty of the enormous lobby overwhelmed her. She excitedly followed him and made a left turn from the hallway. He stopped by a red wood door. She'd never seen anything like it. The apartment had high ceiling and large windows that let in plenty of morning sunlight, illuminating the glamor of the penthouse. Julia had never seen such radiant light before. She noticed so much more than sunlight. She felt the beauty of the universe itself.

She found spark of care inside his eyes, inside their sea of kindness.

"You know," he said, "I inherited a tender Lucia white gold vase from my father. Fragile, beautiful, precious. He always told me to take utmost care of things like that. Rare things. I never understood him, really. Now I do."

He let go of her hand, and she felt a wave of heat leave her body. She wanted him to touch her forever.

"Unfortunately, I have a meeting in about twenty minutes, and have to run. Meanwhile, please, feel free to access anything you need to get cleaned up and warm," he said in a soft voice. He pointed straight ahead of her "The shower is across to your right. There is food for your taking in the kitchen. I will leave the keys and money, right here on this table. If you are able, you can go out to the shop to buy fresh clothes." He gave her a loving glance "Please be here when I return."

Julia wanted to speak, but she felt a lump in her throat. Her mind raced like wind ripping through the pressure of a storm. She uttered a few words. "That is... this... thank you. I don't know how to thank you."

He stepped closer and reached over, as though he was going to caress her cheek, but he stopped and smoothed his hair instead. She was happy he did. She wasn't sure what to make out of the situation. She did know that she was enamored with the apartment which overlooked the streets she knew so well. She liked Jack being next to her too, but if she was honest with herself, she was afraid he was playing a cruel joke. But his words reassured her.

"I have the resources to help you. It feels right to have you with me. Will you wait until I get back? I won't be long." He inched in; his breath so close she felt it on her lips. Her knees buckled. She hoped he didn't notice the trickle of her sweat. Or how she must have smelled. She always tried to take care of herself. Stealing toothbrushes and soap would no longer be a priority if she stayed here. She disliked stealing, but she had no choice. She couldn't recall the last time she'd had a proper bath. She felt a warm blush on her cheeks. She turned away hoping he didn't notice that either. When she caught a glimpse of his familiar smile out of the corner of her eye, she let out a breath.

"Yes, I'll wait." Of course she'd wait. She wouldn't go back to the streets. He seemed trustworthy. No matter how much she questioned his motives, she felt that he was being genuine. Besides if he wanted to harm her, he probably would have. From the mystery books she read in the library, she understood that serial killers didn't situate their women in fancy apartments. But then again, that was fiction.

She waited to explore until the door closed behind him. The sound of her footsteps left an echo in the penthouse. Afraid to touch the polished furniture or sit on the light beige couch, she went back to the entryway by the side table, staring at the white envelope. Taking a few deep breaths to prevent hyperventilation, she regained control of her shaking limbs. Her heart rate dropped to its normal pace and her mind was clear enough to think straight again.

When she saw what was inside the envelope, she dropped it back on the table like it was a hot coal. She'd never seen so many dollar bills in her lifetime. Paper money was the rarest of things to her. She was accustomed to the *clink* of coins, not the shuffling of bills.

She decided to leave the envelope where she found it and take care of her hunger pains. She tiptoed to the kitchen, careful not to touch anything. She found all sorts of delicious goods in Jack's refrigerator. She filled her stomach with the various kinds of food, all of which were plentiful inside the refrigerator. She reached out to grab more but nausea took over. She took a deep breath. As her abdominal muscles contracted, the food splattered the floor next to her dirty feet in a disgusting, foul-smelling pile. She panicked. She had not only managed to dirty the floor with her footsteps, but also managed to stink it up with her vomit. The floor tiles were covered in it. She had to stop herself from hyperventilating. After pulling herself together, she found a washcloth and cleaned up the mess. She opened the windows to let fresh air into the apartment. Wandering around to look for the washroom, she couldn't help but stop now and then to admire Jack's artwork and the furniture. A lot of the work reminded her of the paintings she'd seen only in books.

The two-story penthouse had a lovely terrace area with a view of the city. It claimed eight bedrooms and ten bathrooms, a private entrance with exclusive access to the rooftop terrace which included a sauna, spa, gym, and incredible precious marble throughout. She'd only known that because she'd read about it in the paper. Many buildings that housed servants' quarters were being restructured into fancy homes to suit those wealthy enough to afford them. When Julia had first read the initiative, she'd felt sadness. She'd always hoped that someone would pluck her off the streets and give her a job as a servant. That had been a wild fantasy, or so she had thought.

She tiptoed, as if her very presence in the place would somehow manage to destroy the beauty of it. The kitchen was vast, extravagant, and seemed designed for the use of professional staff. There was also an elegant dining room designed for entertaining large parties, staff quarters, and a security room. With her head spinning, she tried to remember the location of each room.

She turned the knobs of the shower one by one, trying to figure out how to turn on the hot water, how to adjust the cold, and how to keep that thing on the top to stop from sprinkling ice-cold water on her. When she figured it all out, she lowered her bony figure into the bath and melted into the warmth of clean water. She scrubbed her pale skin with a soft cloth. The water alone felt as though it was removing, along with the dirt and grime, the years she'd spent out in the world alone. She wished she could scrub them from her mind as well and they could swirl with all the filth down into the drain. Gone forever. But she couldn't. The horrible memories of her life did not fall away so easily.

Everything felt upside down. She thought she would feel reborn after such a fancy bath, but she felt the opposite. When she settled back into her scruffy clothes, she felt more like herself. She knew she needed to get new clothing. When she held the keys to the penthouse, she felt as though she owned something—something that wasn't a plank of soggy cardboard. She had actual keys, which opened up an actual door. To an actual apartment. Her hands shook as she picked up the envelope. She was well-aware of how much money was inside it, and she needed to keep it close. She tucked the envelope into her clothing, used her new key to lock the apartment door behind her, and walked to the dress shop. The saleswomen gave her funny looks.

"If you want to make sure I'm not here to steal your things, go ahead and follow me. I understand. I'm sure you don't see many women who look like me, do ya? Well, come one then. Follow me around." And they did follow her, but Julia wasn't bothered by it.

When she was rid of her smelly and torn rags inside the shop's dressing room, she felt much different. She even pictured herself in the new clothing, sitting outside the pastry shop across the street, eating desert. She imagined blending in with regular people. She had decided on a cream satin high-neck blouse with a black pleated, A-line wool skirt. She added boots with a small heel, that she had to walk around in to get used to. A warm mink coat wrapped around her body as snug as her mother's embrace. She wished both that she was seven again, back with her parents, and that they could see her now. She wished she could remember more.

As she twirled before the mirror, she saw that she looked just like any one of those women she saw clicking past her in their heels every single day.

She purchased several accessories—gloves, hats, and more shoes. Even after all of those purchases, there was money in the envelope. She thanked the shop assistant as she paid, trying to stabilize her balance, her feet wedged into the stiff boot. She adjusted her dark burgundy bowler hat and made her way to 42nd and Broadway.

She crossed the street and bought herself the biggest, tastiest looking doughnut in the shop.

JACK

He had to see her. Jack rushed to the penthouse as if his life depended on it. He didn't tell his wife he would be late for dinner, or that he might not even be back for dinner. His heart wrenched as he thought of his children. They stood in a frame in his mind, separate from their mother, and there was yet another frame with Julia. He hated himself for what he was doing. He just couldn't see himself in the same frame as the children's mother and he didn't understand why.

The pace of his respirations was too slow. He felt as though he could not move enough air through his lungs, and blood to his heart. Despite the chill in the winter air, he was burning up—sweating. He was in a state of panic, until he reached into his pocket and felt a velvet box. His heart rate slowed back to a normal pulse as he ran his thumb across it—the fabric reminding him of the box's contents. He had bought a gift to present to his new guest.

Once he stepped inside his penthouse, he found Julia sleeping on the living room sofa. He took a deep breath as he sat next to her and studied her features. She had an other-worldly feel. Enchanting. She was like a magnet that drew every inch of his being to hers.

His fingers brushed her cheek, and he noticed a hint of rose color in her pale skin. He pulled his hand back, not wishing to wake her, but it was too late. Her breathing changed, and she opened her eyes to look at him.

"Sorry for waking you," he whispered.

Julia sprang up and drew her knees to her chest. She looked confused, a little scared even.

He needed to stay with her. Comfort her. He needed to love her. His wife and kids. Their images, and his memories of them flicked in and out of his mind. Jack couldn't imagine what had come over him. Why had he stopped caring for his wife that day? His kids were everything to him, his wife—nothing.

SWEET TIMES

JULIA
Winter
Late 1930s

"We were cursed. Doomed to be miserable together. Mostly because I was aware that he never truly loved me. Not many had, other than my parents, and I could not remember them much. I knew no true love of my own. Until I had you."

— A LETTER

"You're back." Julia tried to push aside the array of negative thoughts, and she smiled at him. She resisted the urge to reach over and touch his curls. She was still unsure about him, and she was unsure about how everything between them had unfolded. What did he want from her? She was afraid to say something wrong. To utter a word out of place. She thanked the library books for the words and education she'd received from them alone. She tried to act like one of those well-to-do ladies from one of the romantic books she read. She was still afraid.

Afraid of being in the apartment, even afraid of all the food. And the money. She wanted to hoard all of it. Not spend a penny from what was left in the envelope.

"I couldn't wait to get back. I had to see you again." He placed his hat on the couch. "This came into one of my stores from overseas just yesterday." He removed a velvet box from his pocket and unclipped a strand of pearls before draping them over her hands.

Julia gasped. Her arms were still wrapped, frozen around her knees. She was afraid to let go of them, or the gift. She was terrified that her hands would wander toward the curve of his lips.

"I want to know everything. Everything about you." He leaned in closer. The pleasant smell of cigars and fresh cologne hit her nostrils.

"Well, I don't know much myself." She shrugged.

"What do you mean?"

"I know that I had parents, and that they loved me. They gave me everything in the world. The last memory of them I have is my seventh birthday. They gave me a beautiful locket with the letter "J" inscribed on it. The locket had a message inside. After I received the gift, my parents took me upstate to my grandmother's cottage, and then... I don't remember a thing. I don't know what happened to them. Or to me after that day. I don't remember."

She'd never told a soul her story. Unloading it felt like a brick she'd never known was there had fallen from her shoulders. She held on to a little hope that, maybe if she talked about it, she would remember a little more. Maybe she could start to heal.

"I mean, after traveling upstate with them I recall waking up on the streets. I don't know how or why. It's been twelve hard years, I begged, got by somehow. Nobody wanted to hire me for work, no one even looked my way. It was dangerous at times. People tried to take advantage of me. But I fought. Wish I knew more about what happened to my parents, to me." Julia took a deep breath. "The only thing that kept me going was the library. It was a place to forget about me, and just live another life. Learn something new and exciting."

Jack tilted his head to look at her. Julia watched as a sadness filled his eyes. He got up to pace the living room.

"I wish I could do something to help you remember."

"Me too."

Jack stopped his pacing to look back at her. "I will do anything it takes, all that is within my power to help you live a better life, that's my promise." When he cupped and squeezed her small hands in his, she felt reassured. Julia's heart fluttered as she imagined him doing much more than just touching hands. Her face felt a flush of heat. She pulled away from his touch, even though it was pleasant and warm. She hugged her knees again and looked away from him to the skylight above her.

"Did I offend you?" he asked when her hands dropped to her knees.

She shifted on the French carved oak sofa. "No, no. Not at all. I just need time to adjust, to wrap my mind around what's happening." She wanted to wrap her hands around him and pull him closer to her body. His skin closer to hers. Things she'd never felt before. "Everything seems so magical, that's all."

"It does. And I'm sorry If I'm being too forward, too fast. But I felt as if I had been missing a piece of my life, and now that I have you with me, it's as if I've found it. You are what I want to live for."

Hearing him speak sent shivers all over her body. "After I lost my parents. No one ever cared for me. I always felt so useless and small. Alone. Ready to fight for myself because no one ever fought for me. So, thank you Jack, for caring." She let out a sheepish smile. "What about you? Tell me about yourself." Julia released her hands from her knees.

Jack gathered two glasses from behind the bar to fill with whisky. "Drink?"

"Sure." Julia reached for the beverage.

He handed the glass to her and paced the living room again while holding his own drink as he spoke. "My life revolved around my father and making him happy. My father was a stock market guru and property owner. After he passed away, I was to take over the empire he built. As the only child, I inherited all his hard work. I was blessed with a golden touch I guess, taking over the business tripled its profits. I opened up jewelry stores, bought more properties, and turned to investments." He cleared his throat as if he had more to say, but he stopped.

Instead, he took a deep gulp from his glass. After emptying it, he placed it on the bar counter and took her by the hand, lifting her off the couch. She stumbled into his embrace, her knees buckling again.

"You know what I think?" he whispered, his breath touching her ear. "I think we should get out. Spend the night on the town. Let's have dinner in one of my favorite restaurants." Now his mouth was so close to hers, she could feel his sweet breath.

"Yes," she rasped. He led her to the hallway, she noticed how his long fingers danced as he laced his shoes. She felt a flush of pleasant warmth in places even street ladies don't mention. She didn't know could feel such heat.

She cleared her throat. "Where to?"

"You wait and see, Madam." Jack half-kneeled and tipped his hand, gesturing to the hallway. They made their way through the building. Julia felt like a princess. Dazzled, charmed and enchanting. She didn't allow herself more than a moment of this line of thinking before she tucked it to the recesses of her mind. Closer to the surface than her memories from long ago. This was fresher, almost keepable. Something she hoped she could return to.

Seb'on, an intimate French restaurant, stood in the heart of the wealthy area. They were on 8th and 58th, a part of town Julia never imagined stepping foot inside. She tried to walk like the rest of the ladies, with poise and confidence, but her new shoes didn't cooperate with her feet. Or her lack of confidence.

The host welcomed Jack with a courteous smile. They were seated at once in the not-so-crowded snug paradise at the back of the room. The light cushioned chairs and glowing chandeliers had Julia's mouth agape. A heavenly smell filled the air. A server approached them in haste.

"So sorry for the wait Mr. Roe."

Jack looked at his watch. "It's been only a second, you gotta do better next time." He tried to look serious, then smirked, touching the waiter's shoulder. "Gus, my friend you worry too much. All is perfect." Gus exposed his impressive straight and white teeth in a large grin.

"The usual for me, and Roasted Dublin Bay prawns for the lady," Jack said.

Gus nodded his head and rushed off to the kitchen.

The candle on the table brought a soft comfortable glow, and all Julia could do was smile. The contrast between her life that morning and her life that night was so improbable, but there she was, soaking in the candlelit atmosphere of such a place she couldn't have dreamed of, and with Jack who looked more gorgeous than ever.

Everything he said, the way he looked at her, the way he moved was just how she imagined him in her dreams. He was at least two heads taller than her, and she loved it. He was almost unbelievably kind. She wondered if she'd wake to the cold nightmare of life on the street. If this was all some wonderful dream. Maybe she was lying frozen in a coma. If so, she prayed she'd stay in that coma forever.

"Julia, you are going to love it here. The food is phenomenal." He reached over to touch her hands. This time, she didn't pull away.

"You are so gorgeous. Why didn't I take you in before? What a fool I was, seeing you so frequently and doing so little. How did I not see *you*?" He leaned over, nearly whispering.

"I will show you the world, I will make you the happiest woman on Earth."

She blushed and opened her mouth, but she was speechless. Luckily, she did not have to speak. The waiter returned to their table. She turned her attention to the gold bone china dinner plate set in front of her.

The server presented a bottle of Amour de Deutz. "On the house from Chef Jauk."

"Why thank you. Send my regards," Jack answered.

Gus steadied his hands to open the bottle and poured its contents into their champagne glasses.

Jack spent most of that time staring at Julia while she enjoyed heavenly bites of the most delicious food in the universe.

For dessert, Jack ordered Chocolate de Notre Manufacture. Julia licked her fingers. Jack chuckled.

"You are just too cute. Should I order more?"

"Yes!" Julia exclaimed. "I'm sorry. Yes, please. I'm forgetting my manners," she said, licking the rest of the chocolate from her index finger.

"You got some on your mouth, right there." He leaned across the table to wipe the chocolate off with his thumb. She stopped breathing for a second.

"I can do this. I can definitely do this."

"Do what?" he asked, hand now on hers.

"Eat chocolate while you adore me for the rest of our lives," she blurred out.

His bold laugh left her feeling ashamed. She wanted to puke from embarrassment. "Sorry," she said.

"Not at all. I'm laughing because you are adorable. And I would like nothing more than to see you all my life, happy as you are now."

Julia took a deep breath. The shame she had felt disintegrated. "I want to know more about you Jack." She took a small sip of the champagne.

"Well. There is something you ought to know." He stopped, Julia suspected he wanted to get up and pace as he had back in the penthouse. And he did stand. He gestured for her to follow him, and on their walk, Julia continued to speak. He put a finger to his mouth. Julia was confused only for a moment. He meant to lower the volume of speech.

"Well then?" she whispered as she shifted her weight on her feet, wishing her new shoes didn't feel so tight.

"I adore you, and the more time I spend with you, I adore you even more. But the thing is Julia..." he paused. "How about this; let's take dessert home and I'll tell you everything."

"Home," Julia repeated. "I like how that sounds."

"So do I," Jack said as he collected their coats from the coat clerk. They stepped outside. The wind played samba with his red curls. And Julia loved watching it. Everything about him, and how the environment around him played with his appearance, movements, and features.

When they were in the car, on their way back to the penthouse, Julia noticed how oddly quiet Jack had become. She had a bad feeling as she wondered what he was thinking. Maybe he wanted to get rid of her already? He seemed trustworthy but far more extravagant in living than she was used to. She was still a little afraid of the whole turn of events. Even so, even if only for one day, this was better than the streets. But the clothing, was uncomfortable. Her new tights were itchy, her boots squeezed every one of her toes, and the mink coat seemed to pull her body down with its weight. Julia purposefully thought of everything she could that was negative about her current situation. After all, it was too good to be believed. Something bad was in the air. Maybe she had been a fool.

When they walked inside the penthouse, she made herself appear comfortable on one of the kitchen stools. Jack laid out the chocolate and whisky on the bar table.

"Well?" she questioned again, reaching for one of the chocolate bars. She felt much more relaxed around him now. But she was still wary.

"The thing is, Julia, I'm married," he blurted.

She pulled her hand back, deciding against the sweet treat. Her eyes fell toward the floor. The old woman's words repeated in her head: *"He's married, and has a family of his own, you will never be happy."*

"Frankly, I don't know what to do with myself. I feel torn. I want to be with you, and only you. But at the same time, I don't know how I will leave them. My children, three of them." He held his breath and gulped his whisky. He paced, again, from one giant corner of the living room to the next.

Julia tried to control her breathing. Her heart rate jumped the same way it had when she was thirteen years old, and she thought the police would catch and arrest her for stealing a doughnut. Yet, she managed to stay composed. She slid off the stool. "Jack, we will figure something out," she said in a tone so calm, she surprised herself. She hadn't expected to say such a thing herself. She was used to fleeing when she was scared or uncertain. Instead, she felt compelled to stay right where she was. Right near Jack.

"Will we?" His jaw tightened. "I'm not sure if we will. I don't know what came over me, truly. Very, surprising thing, you see?"

"May I offer a solution?" Julia found herself taking the initiative. She wanted Jack and this life more than anything she'd wanted for a while. She hadn't had much time to *want* anything. Not on the streets. Just need after need being met, if only enough to survive. She looked to Jack. He nodded in response to her question, and she continued.

"I can stay here, and you can visit me. Until you are ready. I mean, ready to leave them. For us."

She found Jack staring into space and felt foolish, impulsive enough to touch his shoulder. "Do you want to go to them now?"

"No. I want to stay by your side. Always."

A satisfied grin spread across her face. "Whatever you wish."

The rest of the night, they spoke about Julia's rough days on the streets. Julia could see that Jack was head over heels for her. She tried to steer away from any conversation about his wife and children. She noticed how his mind traveled far away, and he fell silent when she mentioned them. She hated talking about them too, and very much hated that expression of his that meant he was elsewhere—with them and not her.

Jack played with her hair while she studied his large hands and long fingers. She also noticed his broad shoulders and imagined him sweeping her off the couch and carrying her to the bedroom. Devouring him with her eyes, she stared into his sparkling blue eyes. They radiated kindness and joy. He soothed her heart. His presence functioned as a tranquilizer, and she drifted into a sweet calm sleep. The kind of sleep she had only experienced as a little girl, with her parents by her side. When she was seven years old.

She woke up in strange, large bed. It was the first time she could remember sleeping in a bed for many years. She was fully clothed and was rather comfortable. She felt as though she had slept on a cloud. She was covered with goose feather blankets and surrounded by fluffy pillows. Three white orchids, a box of chocolates, and a note lay on one of the pillows.

Dearest Julia. You are such a charm. I cannot wait to see you again. Unfortunately, I had to attend business conventions early this morning and did not want to wake you. You are such a peaceful sleeper.

Also, unfortunate, is that I must travel out of the city. I must see my family tonight. I will try to phone you as soon as I get the chance. I have left an envelope for you on the dining room table. Please feel free to buy whatever your heart desires. I hope you enjoy what's in the box. It made me think of you. It's delicate and one of its kind. I'm looking forward to our next meeting." Always yours, and always with you.

—Jack.

Julia crumpled the letter into a small ball and threw it across the room. She displayed the body language of a child—pouty with her arms crossed on her chest. She wanted Jack with her. She wished she could stay in bed forever, with him but he had gone away. She picked up the small velvet box from the pillow and opened it to find a pear-shaped pearl pendant with a large diamond in the middle.

Julia sprang out of bed and looped the gold chain around her neck before she walked to the mirror to admire it on her flesh.

A fresh cup of hot coffee was a different start to the day than what she was used to. The clothes she purchased the day before hung nearby. As she dressed, she told herself that someday, Jack would belong only to her, just like the new clothes.

THE DECISION

JULIA

She loved summers. they were, happy and free, and they reminded her of vacationing in Virginia with her parents

She took extra care in putting herself together. It was her 21st birthday, and Jack had promised to take her somewhere special after he finished with his family dinner.

Julia waited for him in the penthouse. She always waited for him with great patience. Waited for him to leave his family for her. Waited until they could be themselves, as a couple in public. She hoped to welcome Jack with a little show of cleavage. She ran her hands along her black and gold cocktail dress, smoothing it until it satisfactorily complimented her shape.

Resting on the penthouse balcony was peaceful. Julia rocked on the stool next to the side table where she kept her gloves. A red cashmere scarf shielded her from the summer night's breeze. She didn't care that the soft wind fussed with her hair, her mind raced to other things. It flooded with questions that only time could answer.

As she stared at the lonely, fresh orchids and chocolates through the glass doors, she decided to get up and walk through the door. Once there, she picked up her favorite treat. Only a few days had passed since Jack brought her the delightful flowers on his latest visit, but it seemed like much more time had passed.

Chocolate will never let me down, she told herself as she popped the sweet square in her mouth, enjoying its rich taste. As she reached for another, the telephone rang. She drew her hand back from the chocolate and grabbed the telephone.

"Hello?"

"Ms. Julia, this is Benjamin from downstairs. Mr. Roe is awaiting your presence outside."

"Yes, yes I'll be right there!" She dropped the phone and ran to the mirror to reapply her lipstick. She put on her pearl necklace and earrings.

She admired the way her long, dark, and thick locks fell over her shoulders. Her makeup was perfect, her skin was smooth, and her figure thin. Her confidence shone through her smile.

Foggy memories of her parents came back to her. Vaguely, she remembered her seventh birthday party and how her parents gave her the special locket with their pictures in it and the scribble on the back of their photos which read *Pure love breaks pure evil.*

The only person who the answers Julia needed was the old lady she'd encountered so long ago, but she hadn't been able to find her anywhere since. She remembered the way her mother hugged her tight and soothed her after a bad dream.

But this night was her twenty-first birthday, and Julia wanted to enjoy it without thinking about the past.

Collecting her silver clutch, and putting on pearly pumps, she closed the door behind her in anticipation of seeing Jack.

It was much warmer downstairs than out on the balcony. Jack was standing by the car holding out three orchids.

"You look amazing," he said. Her dress had the effect she'd intended; he looked as if he wanted to have her right then. She hoped he wanted to rip her dress off as soon as they were inside the car. But a formal lady waits as long as possible. It was frustrating. Because he was married, Jack wasn't ready. There was a push and pull that was strong between them. Both of equal intensity and weight.

"Why thank you Mr. Roe." Julia brushed her lips against his.

"Are you ready to go?" he asked.

"When I'm with you. I'm always ready." She meant that in more ways than one.

Jack gave her a soft kiss. He opened the back door to the Rolls Royce and welcomed her inside the cab.

"I have something extraordinary planned for us."

"So I've heard! I cannot wait."

He slid onto the white leather seat next to her and signaled the driver the go-ahead.

"Where are we going?" she asked, tapping her knees.

"Dinner," Jack replied with a sly smile.

"I know that smile, Jack. You're hiding something aren't you?"

"Whatever gave you that idea?" He laughed and wrapped her hands in his. She noticed how he shivered with need. How his eyes burned with desire. He released her hands too quickly for her liking and looked off into the distance. He had gone to that far-away place.

Julia stiffened her upper lip and attempted to hold back tears. She turned to face the window. It bothered her that he avoided more intimate physical contact. Sometimes it made her feel as filthy as she had on the streets. Worse. Dirty and unwanted. Unwanted by the man who said he loved her. Sometimes the cruelty of the situation hurt her more than she thought she could take.

It helped to think that he needed more time to get used to their relationship, with his family in the way and all.

She turned to him. "Ok, if you're not hiding anything, then I know where we are going. *Seb'on*," she stated.

"You'll just have to wait and see, love."

It was Saturday night, and people drifted through the congested bright-lit Manhattan streets. The Broadway theatres were full of couples who always looked to be in love. Like a best friend, the city had a way to warm Julia's heart. Their car passed the buzzing streets of Manhattan, jumping onto the highway toward Long Island. *Seb'on* was left behind.

"Love, we've passed our favorite restaurant," Julia said, not bothering to hide her confusion.

"Yes, dear. But today, we are going elsewhere." Jack signaled for the driver to switch lanes.

The car rolled off the busy highway and proceeded through the silent streets of long Island, where it came to a stop. To her right was an enormous black and gold gate that led to what looked like a castle. The spiral staircases on both sides lead to the front door, whose beauty was accentuated by a tall regal water fountain in the middle of the U-shaped driveway.

Jack took Julia's small hand in and led her to the entrance of the mansion.

"This is a beautiful hotel." The four-story tower reminded her of the things of fairy tales, the ones her mother used to read to her before bedtime. "They must have an amazing restaurant here. I bet it's better than *Seb'on*."

Jack's face shone. He led her to the double doors. Julia admired the exquisite stained glass, the sharply arched windows, vaulted ceilings, and ornate furnishings that played to the mansion's grand appearance.

She also noticed that no one was around to check them in. "It's so quiet here. What kind of hotel is this?"

"This is not a hotel, love."

They ascended another set of staircases and took a slight right onto a balcony. Colorful orchids sat on a small round table with a white tablecloth, radiating in the soft light.

"Dinner in a beautiful castle." She clapped her hands, stepping around the balcony to admire the view of the estate. A vast garden stared back at her. Every tree was decorated with thousands of small lights playing with the moonlight above them.

She heard him come close, felt his hands cover her eyes. They had the delicate feel of rose petals.

"Happy birthday, love. This is not an ordinary birthday, you know? I want you to make a decision today, but keep your eyes closed!"

She obeyed. When she felt his hands leave her eyes, her heart raced. She jumped up and down, so excited, she babbled. "It must have cost you a fortune to rent this place for us."

"Turn around and open your eyes," he said in a whisper.

Jack was on the ground. On one knee. He smiled from ear to ear, hands slightly trembling. Something in his eyes danced.

She brought her palms to her mouth to prevent a loud gasp. He held out a sparkling sapphire diamond ring, inlaid with smaller diamonds around it and within its silver band.

"Are you ready to be Mrs. Roe?"

Her mid raced as she wondered when, or if, he'd filed for divorce but thought the timing was terrible for her to ask such a thing. The moment was perfect, and she loved and wanted Jack too much to ruin such a beautiful moment.

"Yes. Of Course, I want to. More than life itself." She stopped for a moment to wipe a tear.

He slipped the ring on her finger and kissed her hand. "The divorce paperwork came back. It's just me and you now. And one day you will meet my children too."

"Divorced?"

He ignored her wide-eyed, open-mouthed expression and he led her to a table set with fine china. His smile was bigger than it had been before. "All of this," he said swinging his palms as if to wrap the mansion within in his large hands, "this is for you."

"I know you did all this for me. Thank you for making my birthday perfect. You are a brilliant man. I knew I loved you before I even met you."

"I love you too. More than I thought possible. I will make us happy. I promise." He stretched his hands to touch hers, his skin flushed. Was he thinking what she was thinking?

"When I said this was all for you, I meant this is your new home. *Our* new home. This house is your early wedding gift from me."

She took large gulps of wine from her glass then attempted a deep breath, but the air felt stiff and tight. Her lungs seemed to freeze. Julia gasped to take in the scents around her. The soft hint of citrus and the smell of the orchids warmed her. She looked down at her ring finger. The diamond glittered in the light of the moon. "I'm the happiest ex-homeless orphan in the world right now." After emptying her glass, she circled her arms around his neck.

She no longer wanted to wait for him to make the big move. She didn't even have to think about it, as her hands traveled to his mouth and her finger caressed his lips. His mouth curved into a pleasant smile, as she practically dove into him in for a kiss. Her heart raced she wanted him all, in body and mind. All to herself.

The wine did its job, her limbs felt warm and wobbly, her mind rode upon a soft calm wavelength. Never having known a man the way she wanted to know Jack at that very moment didn't stop her from landing kisses all over his face. As she let instinct take over, she fell into his arms. His kisses felt like clouds against her lips. His hands traveled to her shoulders and then to her back to untie the strings of her dress. As the fabric fell away from her breasts, Jack pulled back to admire her for a moment. His hands caressed her bare breasts, a small moan escaped her lips. Shivering at the unknown, she peered into his gracious blue eyes. She recognized a look of reassurance, and the fear melted from her body as she waited for another one of his tender strokes. She trembled as he pressed his lips harder against hers

"Do you want me to stop?" he whispered, warm breath on her lips.

"Never."

His hands traveled to her flat belly, and his fingers danced around her belly button. Her body flushed with heat. Anticipation tingled down to her toes.

"I want you, Julia." Her heart skipped beats when she heard the words. He lifted her in his arms and carried her inside, through the enormous palace into to a bedroom. Next to a lit fireplace, he laid her down on a large flokati sheepskin rug. Now above her, he gave her a million tiny kisses, traveling down to most sacred places. She tried lifting him to her to taste his lips once again. He complied and their mouths met. Her hands moved down to feel him.

"Yes," a needy groan escaped his lips. He moved from her belly button down in between her thighs.

She lay with her body dancing at his commands, allowing him to do as he willed, brushing her hands through his messy red curls, she kissed him over and over. Now, beyond herself, she needed him.

"Am I hurting you?" He stooped to peer into her eyes.

She shook her head. "No. Don't stop, I want to feel you forever."

He moved inside her slowly, penetrating the depth of her very being, sharing a piece of himself. He did not take his eyes off her.

Something magical happened at that moment, her insides began to shiver with bliss. Her thoughts were elsewhere, in some heavenly realm. She was overcome by every minuscule, physiological detail of euphoria ever known to mankind. And this collection of paradise and ecstasy erupted, releasing every fiber of negative energy she held within.

She watched him, moving atop her, his eyes closed, and his deep groans grew louder until he collapsed next to her, cradling her in his arms. She felt so close to, and in love with, him at that moment.

༄

"Didn't I tell you, silly girl? Your happiness will come with a price. I hear true love does not come easily."

Julia felt some sort of cloud around her silky, combed hair—something that set each hair on end. Then it encompassed her entire body. The cloud was invisible, but it felt heavy, like a million pounds just weighing her down. And it carried that horrid, screechy voice.

"Ooh, you smell good girl, no more rags hah?"

"I will take your firstborn child for payment," the voice hissed, with a subtle fade, and it kept repeating.

༄

Julia jumped out of bed in a sweat, waking her fiancé.

"What is it, my love?" Jack asked, still half asleep.

"Just a dream, that's all. Just a dream, go back to sleep,"

Jack turned to his left and closed his eyes. She fluffed her pillow, but she could not get comfortable. She could not fall asleep. She knew too well that her happiness was not destiny, but a payment.

"Jack." She shook him from his sleep. "I can't sleep. I can't do this anymore."

He sat up rubbing his eyes. "What is it, love?"

"I have these dreams and this monstrous fear."

He wrapped his hands around her, still drowsy. "What dreams?"

Julia cleared her throat. "Well. This might sound crazy..." she hesitated. "I-I have dreams about a witch. They come pretty often. The dreams.

And they will not allow me to rest. The witch tells me your love isn't real. And I'm afraid she's right."

Jack clasped her hands tighter and kissed her knuckles. "No. Love, those are just dreams. I love you, you know that. I divorced my wife for goodness' sake. It will break my kids' hearts, for us Julia. All this for us."

"I know. But there is something you don't know." She took her hands from his and huffed. "This will definitely sound crazy." She twirled her engagement ring. "The witch, she's real. And if it wasn't for her, you would have never rescued me, let alone ask me to marry you."

He laughed. "My sweet, sweet Julia. How wrong you are. You think this is too good to be true, but it isn't. My love cannot be explained away. Not even by witches or warlocks, or any evil you can think of." He cupped her small face in his palms, as he brushed his soft lips against hers.

"Jack, I know how I must sound, but she is real." Julia tried to stop him from showering her with kisses.

"Those are just dreams, my love, mere dreams." His kisses traveled to her neck and shoulders, and she melted into his embrace. "This," he trailed his hands down her arms and whispered in her ear, "this is real."

"I don't ever want to lose you Jack Roe. Or share you with anyone ever again."

"You will never lose me, my love." he grinned, letting his fingers dance between her thighs.

POWER UNEARTHED

ANGELA
Fall
Early 1970s

One thing I did know; you would be taken from me. And there would be little I could do to stop it. Please forgive me. There was an unknown clock ticking away, somewhere, the seconds with which I would spend with you. If I could find that device, I would destroy it with all my might.

I wish I knew what would become of you, or me.

That witch will continue to haunt us because she seeks access to eternity, and we are the channel through which her iniquitous ship can sail to reach it.

— A LETTER

It was Sunday, her day off. The sun was extra bright, and it glared through the window into Angela's eyes as she stretched in bed. She looked at the time. Ten in the morning. She loved that she slept in late.

Last night's pleasant encounter flashed in her mind. Caiden. She smiled. Caiden had told her the night before that he wanted to meet with her tonight. When the telephone rang, she expected to hear Liam's voice, but it was Robert from the studio.

"Hi Angela. I think I can help with your memory. I know how you needed to take time off and all. But there is a developing story. They want to put the intern on it, and he won't handle it well. Not as well as you. If you get back on coverage maybe that would help. You know? How about it?" He sounded nervous. She could imagine the sweat trickling down his round face.

She thought about it. The idea of working near that man did not appear to her. "Well, I'm not sure. How can I be better than the intern if I don't know what I'm doing?" She considered for a moment that she may actually know what she was doing. She'd been on the Roe case and maybe this story was similar. She just didn't know how to behave in front of a camera.

He pressed further. "All right then. How 'bout you come meet us and you see how it's done?"

"What time are you and the intern leaving the studio?"

"About an hour from now."

"If I'm not there within an hour, you'll just know I decided against it."

"Take the address down. They are having a rally for the new election, and we got lead from a rat that the rally will not go as planned."

"Sound's interesting." Something crossed her mind the way her memories did here and there, but it was excitement. She remembered being excited about reporting and covering new stories. "I think I might take you up on the offer," she blurted before hanging up. As soon as she put the receiver down, the phone rang again.

She picked it up. "Angela Wise," she answered. That was new. Was that how she'd usually answered the phone?

"Angela. It's Caiden. I hope this isn't too odd, but I never got your number the other night, so I asked Liam for it. He said you wouldn't mind, so..." he trailed off.

"Hello, Caiden. No, no that's great," she said. Her words were quick, and she felt a tinge of embarrassment that he could likely sense her enthusiasm.

"So, I was thinking, how about I swing by now? Like, maybe for some coffee?" There was just the smallest hint of a strain in his voice, like he was nervous to ask.

Angela closed her eyes and tapped the phone against her forehead. She wished he'd called her before Robert had. "I can't until tonight. I'm going down to the studio. To learn from an intern." It sounded worse than it felt.

"I see. Busy bee, huh? Ok, well, we're still on for tonight, aren't we?"

"Absolutely, I can't—" she cut herself off. "I, uh, I'm sorry. I'm looking for a file I can't find. Got distracted." *I can't wait* is what she almost said. "But yeah, I'll see you later."

After wrapping up the call, she prepared to head to work. She arrived at the studio half an hour later, and Robert wasn't there. This was both a relief and an annoyance. She hung her purse on the coatrack near the entrance. She looked for the intern as well. No luck. Upon returning to her office, she figured she'd do her work alone. But she wasn't alone.

To her surprise, Caiden sat across from her desk, waiting for her. There were two cups of coffee on the table next to him.

"Caiden! What are you doing here?" Angela knew she was forgetting something—to feel confused and flustered. To her surprise, the sudden meeting had a smooth and casual feel.

He smiled and stood up, handing her one of the cups of coffee. "I didn't really want to wait for our date. And I know you're busy, but I thought that, if you had the time, maybe we can have a coffee together now, and a dinner date later?"

She chuckled. "Ok. But I gotta go to the Federal Plaza first. They're having a rally there"

"Oh, that's right. The elections. How exciting. It's ok if I come with?"

She didn't have to think before she answered. "Sure."

"Let's take the train. The street traffic will be out of this world with that rally," he suggested.

The two left the newsroom and went to catch the train.

Once they were at the plaza, it was hard for Angela to spot her crew. There were hundreds of people, and reporters. Caiden wrapped his fingers around hers, and they pushed their way through the crowd to the front. They were stopped by a barricade of police officers.

Angela leaned forward just enough that the police wouldn't think she was trying to jump the barricade. Finally, she saw someone familiar. "There. I see Robert," she shouted over the loud noise. She waved her hand and jumped a few times in place in an attempt to get Robert's attention. It was no use. There were too many people, too many reporters on the steps of the Plaza.

"We're with Channel 20 news," she heard Caiden say to one of the police officers.

"ID?" the officer asked monotonously.

Angela had been in such a hurry that morning, she hadn't thought to grab her press ID. "Oh no. This is going to sound like a lie, but I left mine at home. I really did."

The officer shook his head. "Can't let you in, then. Gonna have to run back home to get it."

Caiden stood next to Angela and cut in. "Don't you recognize her? She's Angela Wise. You gotta let us through, she has a story to cover."

The shouting from the crowd grew louder. It rang in Angela's ears, loud and unavoidable. She wanted to make it stop. She released her hand from Caiden's to put her hands over her ears and close her eyes. The crowd seemed to close in on her. When she opened her eyes,

Caiden was no longer next to her. The ringing in her ears continued to get louder. The officer they'd spoken with was unmoving in his stance, it seemed. There were also many people trying to get past the barricade to whom he had to attend. The crowd continued pushing forward, almost knocking Angela off her feet. They shouted for the man who took the podium, the president. And booed his opponent. She tried to stand on her tiptoes to see if she could spot Caiden or Robert. But there were so many faces. So many bodies crammed together. As she searched, a series of loud bangs erupted, and the sound from the crowd swarmed in her mind like a million bees buzzing.

"Caiden!" she yelled now at the top of her lungs. She could barely make out his voice when he called back to her. She couldn't take the noise. Her head throbbed, banging like a hammer against a wall. The bangs were what she assumed to be gun shots. The chaos, the panic, it had to stop. Stop. STOP.

And it did. It all stopped. Everything froze. Everyone was lifeless. The policeman's mouth hung open, and his eyes had a feral, panicked look to them. Some of the people in the crowd still had tears in their eyes, while others were frozen midair, mid-jump, mid-duck, and yet more were lying or crouching on the ground. But no one moved. Nothing moved. The air had a stillness she had never experienced. She moved through the crowd like a mouse in a maze. But much slower. Hear heart thumped so fast she worried it could explode and she'd die right then and there.

Had she stopped time? Or was she imagining it? She brushed it off as best she could. Told herself that she was imagining a frozen scene, even though she could still hear Caiden's voice calling for her. It was coming from the back of the crowd. She rushed across, around, over, and under the motionless bodies. She couldn't help but notice the details of the people, and the collection of them. It was almost beautiful, like a painting of wild animals. And then she found Caiden. He was standing with his arms up, his tall body elongated, his mouth open in a round O.

She got up on her tiptoes and traced her fingers around his. She studied the details of his bumpy nose, his thick brows, and his long dark lashes. She was calm and forgot about the scene around them. She saw him take a small breath and noticed his index finger twitched. The other bodies around her displayed light movements as well. She searched for the bullets. Fast. No time. She spotted one mid-air, then another, and another, all in one disordered line. One of them was so close to a woman's arm. Instinctively, Angela lightly blew on the bullet, and it fell to the ground with a *clink*. There was another twitch from Caiden, and similar twitches from a man close to Caiden's feet. She noticed another bullet headed toward the President, and another toward Robert. More movement filled the corners of her eyes. She realized that everything would be back to its full motion soon.

Angela sprinted to the front, squeezing between the police officers and up the steps. She was inches away from the president. And the bullet. And the bodyguards. She took a deep breath and blew at that bullet, too. *Clink*. To the ground. The president's eyes moved, and Angela ducked, then ran to Robert, where she blew another bullet to the floor. People were moving more. She saw more breathing and twitching, but they remained in a quasi-state of suspended animation. She ran as fast as she could down the steps between the officers, and she ran as fast as she could back to Caiden.

She didn't know how to wake him, so she tried just what she would if she were trying to wake someone from a slumber. She called him quietly. "Caiden," she whispered in his ear. "I'm here. It's Angela. Caiden." She heard a breath, and then another. His arms fell to his sides. His eyes met hers. He didn't seem to notice the stillness around them, the quiet. The world reanimated.

"Angela! Are you ok? Gun shots. Run!" He took her hand as the chaos resumed. He managed to push through some of the crowd. Angela couldn't keep up. He was too fast, and she was too confused, too weak. Something had happened to her. Her knees gave up, refusing to follow commands sent from her brain to just run. Her limbs trembled and her head spun. Caiden must have felt she was in trouble. He scooped her up into his arms and ran.

Angela's head fell on to his shoulder, and her eyes closed. Her mind slowed down.

"We're almost safe. Almost safe," she heard him say. More shots rang out.

"The cameras."

"What?"

"The cameras, I think they were running."

She wanted to go home, cover herself with blankets, and sleep. Her body experienced a significant drop in strength, almost in totality. Her eyes closed again.

When she awoke, she and Caiden were stopped in a car. She must have slept on the way home as well. When Caiden helped her out of the cab, she felt better. She was able to stand up and walk to the front door. Caiden held on to her elbow to support her as they moved through her home.

"You ok?"

"Yeah. You?"

"I am. When I lost you in that crowd..." he placed his hands behind his neck. "Oh gosh, I got scared. Afraid something happened to you."

"I'm fine. I can't believe that happened, and we were there. *Right* there."

"I'm just glad you're ok. You need a drink of water. I can grab you some. Where's the kitchen?"

Angela pointed. "Across the hall, to the right."

"Thank you."

Caiden returned with two glassed of ice-cold water. He handed one to Angela and gulped down one of his own. "I don't understand why anyone would want to assassinate our president."

Angela finished her water and exhaled. "I don't know. I'm just glad we're safe. I'm going to make a phone call to the studio, make sure Robert and the intern are ok." Before going for the phone, she walked to the television and turned on the news. Every news channel was reporting on the incident. Apparently, the president was safe, and the shooter was still at large. No casualties. Angela held her breath, hoping that cameras stopped with time as well. Hoping no one saw her move around the still bodies, bringing down bullets with her breath. Angela still didn't know if she believed that herself.

She made her call to the studio and found out that Robert and the intern were safe. She relayed this information to Caiden.

"And I guess, for some reason, every camera cut out for around twenty minutes. Isn't that weird?" She started fidgeting with her clothing. She didn't feel like she was a good liar. She was, however, relieved about the cameras. No matter what came of those cutting out, she was grateful.

"Yeah, that's unusual, but we should be grateful for the stuff that matters. Truthfully, I'm just glad you didn't get hurt today." His eyes seemed to spark when he looked at her.

"You're staring," she said.

"I have a good reason."

She didn't mind when he studied her. She liked his attention. He cleared his throat and turned away, but she still saw the longing in his eyes.

"I think it's best we stay in today. You ok if we order out and continue our date here?" he asked.

After all that had happened, Angela felt safer inside. "I would love that. But if all our dates start off this way, I might have to cancel on you a few times."

"In my humble opinion, I couldn't care less how our dates start off." He leaned in a little closer, closing his lips to hers. She let him.

They stayed up talking until the sky turned a pinkish orange, and Caiden left in those early morning hours. She wanted to tell him about all the strange things that had happened. The still time, the man turning into a woman back in Liam's apartment building, about seeing herself in a dark awful forest with a snake on her shoulder. She wanted someone to listen to her and tell her that she would be ok. That she'd probably just lost her mind a little after the accident. She wanted someone to tell her she is normal. But of course, she couldn't say those things. Not to Caiden. Not yet at least.

She must have gotten only one hour of sleep when she was woken by the telephone.

"Hey there, Angela, are you ready to do this?" she heard Liam's voice on the other line.

"Do what?" Angela asked, yawing.

"You sound fresh and dandy. The wall. Are you ready to get that thing down? Plus, I didn't have a chance to speak with you yesterday. I must tell you something important. I'll be there in about two hours if you're up for it."

"Oh! The wall. How could I have forgotten? Of course I'm ready. I'll see you soon."

Angela stretched her arms. A smile widened across her face. She looked out the window to the gardens. The birds sang their usual midmorning song. This was one of the happiest days she'd had since she awoke at Liam's after her accident. All she could think of was Caiden.

She went down the staircase into the kitchen. Most of the dust was wiped clean, and the mansion looked at least like someone lived there. She made herself a cup of strong coffee, hoping it would help her recover from too many glasses of wine from the night before.

As she was putting sugar in her cup, a sharp pain shot through her eyes. She felt like her brain had cracked in half. Then she felt light-headed. As a soft, cotton like blackness spread from the corners of her eyes, she felt she would be sick. She managed to rest a hand on one of the kitchen stools to steady herself. And exactly as the doctor had predicted months ago, from nowhere, her memories hit her in a mind-bending instant. She ran across the hall to the living room couch, one hand on her forehead as her head pounded and her and her memories fell upon her brain like cards atop one another in an endless stack.

She hated this mansion. She remembered Zilda, and the magic, and how she'd moved out, How Zilda had told her about her real parents. She understood what the third eye on the woman who had kidnapped her was. What it meant. Everything expanded and then collapsed in on her. Her world widened then restricted. Without the amnesia, she suddenly understood that she had limitations. She was much freer when she didn't know, and the memories just kept coming. Some in the sequential manner she'd hoped for. Angela had magical abilities.

And she wasn't allowed to use them.

NEW BEGINNINGS

ZILDA
Summer
Late 1960s

...if you're reading this, you're either a very precocious youngster, or you've managed to escape your fate. I always had faith that you could do so. I knew that you were stronger than me. Better than me.

The only way to stop the witch is to defeat her. Forever. And I can offer no guidance for you as to how to do so. I apologize for this as well. But truly, I believe you are stronger than I ever was, brighter, kinder.

—A LETTER

Aside from dust in most of the rooms, the mansion hadn't changed much under Zilda's ownership. One major difference was in the kitchen. Massive numbers of glass bottles, one on top of another, filled the kitchen cabinets and shelves. They were transparent and held different sorts of oddities. One of them, for example, had a bull's horn marinating in some sort of greenish liquid. Another housed a few tiny eyes belonging to mice. A couple of large jars held venomous snakes.

Ash looked for tea among the bottle and jar stacks. "Mama I'm going to the store to get some groceries. And tea," she called out from the kitchen, brushing her red locks from her brow.

"Hold on a minute, darling," Zilda said. "What about your lesson?"

"Mama." Ash galloped to the study, kissing Zilda on the forehead and wrapping her in a tight hug around her small frame. "If I don't go to the store, who will take care of you and cook for you?" Her dimples added a soft edge to her smile.

"How many times have I told you that to keep a good figure, you must eat a healthy diet. I have everything we need in that giant kitchen. Just look at you, full-figured, messy red-headed girl. Your lessons are more important than food I say."

Zilda stood and twirled, showing off her tiny waist and she brushed her fingers through her thick, long platinum blonde waves. "This is the figure to keep."

"Mama. I don't feel like having a snake today," Ash joked.

"Girl, you know those jars are for our lessons. We have food in the fridge."

"Mama, you are beautiful in every way, and I'm going to make you something scrumptious." Ash smiled once more and gave Zilda another long hug, then she walked over to the floor-to-ceiling windows. "Why are the drapes covering the beautiful sun again? The windows in this mansion are massive for a reason. Let's get some light in here." Ash pulled back the lengthy dark drapes to let in the sunshine.

"You know I despise light, girl." Zilda blocked her eyes with her palms. "And don't be so nice. How many times am I going to teach you that the world is not full of—"

"Pink-colored unicorns," Ash finished for her with a sigh. "I'm seventeen Mama, let me enjoy the pink unicorns while I can." She ran to the entryway. "Be back in an hour!" she called out.

Ash wasn't making life on Earth any easier for Zilda. It proved difficult to be a mother to a human. In her world, below the earth, their kin went straight to Delirium for training.

A small bird landed on a tree branch by the open window, Zilda whooshed it away, frowning.

Zilda's task seemed impossible. Ash was too pure—too happy—to be taught anything that was impure. Zilda took a deep breath and walked over to the mirror. Seventeen years had passed, and she still looked like a fresh, ripe apple, plucked straight from the tree. Young, vibrant, full of energy, beautiful. Unfortunately, her youth wouldn't last. Unless she drained Ash's soul from her for her eternity. Just a little more time and she was bound to do it. Waiting this long for Ash was like hitting the jackpot. If she had taken the girl's life when she was only seven years old, Zilda would have remained young forever. But taking her life as an adult, with magic flowing in her veins—that would open the path for her kind. Delirium would pick Zilda as his favorite. Then they would occupy the filthy earth and make it their own. She just needed Ash to know a little more magic. An Ortor with fresh magic in her veins, to a witch, was like one pill to cure and prevent all ills to humanity.

Zilda walked over to the kitchen and stared at a jar of maggots. She missed their taste. Living under the same roof with the young creature was torture. Ash seemed untrainable. She was too kind. Nauseatingly nice.

Zilda had tried everything, mostly force, and anger, but Ash always calmed the fire, with a hug here, some dinner there, a laugh, a cuddle.

Zilda placed her hand over her heart. A sharp pain struck her chest, squeezing around the thumping muscle. "Don't fail me, human heart. Do not weaken for the disgusting Ortor," she said to the empty room. "I will have my eternity. I can't fail the underworld. I cannot fail Delirium."

Zilda picked up a jar with three large spiders and went back to the study. She got the tools needed for Ash's lesson. The jar of spiders, candles, cards, a small knife, and a glass of water.

Zilda twisted the knife in her hands, smiling at the thought of Ash's potential for powers. The girl possessed Ortor magic that was stronger than any Ortor she had seen. The more magic in her blood, the better. Teaching Ash to use dark magic was a bonus. Her veins would be sick with it. Ortors only used their powers to kill her kind—dark witches— off, never did they use them for their own benefit.

CAGED BIRD

ASH

Pure love breaks evil. These are the only words my parents left for me.

Never practice magic if you haven't already. It poses a grave danger to you and to your family. Do not use your Ortor powers. If you do, it will ignite that pure evil to ascend from below and ensconce the earth in its rot."

— A LETTER

Ash took in a deep breath of fresh air. The sun shone on her smooth skin, hugging her with a warm welcome. The salted scent of the ocean seasoned the air. Ash closed her eyes wishing she were at the beach, maybe with friends or even her mama. A sad frown spread across her bowtie lips, engulfing her delicate features as she lamented yet again that she hadn't seen much outside the mansion, except Mr. Al's supermarket a few miles down.

It was liberating, getting out of the house, even for twenty minutes. She felt strangled by all the lessons her mama tried to teach her. Like moving objects and turning water to blood. "This will teach you how to manipulate for your personal gain," her mama would say. "This will teach you to read minds. A great tool, to get people to do whatever it is you want." Ash wondered if other people found these types of lessons interesting. She personally found them to be dragging, and an over-whelming bore.

"You are not like other people. You are special. The lessons are special. Do not use your magic unless I tell you that you must."

Ash didn't want to be special; she wanted to be normal. Go to school, have friends, enjoy the beach, discover the world.

To stretch time, she drove at a creeping pace. As she turned right into Al's Supermarket, she waited in the car and listened to the radio before entering the store. Once she was inside, she picked up groceries and made sluggish strides through the small aisles.

"Hey, Mr. Lee." She smiled, as she reached the cashier.

The man brightened. "Ash. Long time no see. Looking radiant as usual."

"Thank you." She chuckled, and a soft hue of red blossomed in her cheeks.

"I was busy learning with Mama. She says homeschooling is the way to go."

Mr. Lee nodded. "Well, she just might be right. Look at you, a very smart young lady. I can't even keep up with talking to you about history, art, politics any of that. You're miles ahead of me. Very smart indeed you are. Maybe you ought to talk to my kiddos, teach them a thing or two. They're in their first year of high school, not doing too well."

"Mr. Lee, I'm not half of what you say. And I really, really wish I could help out, but Mama is so strict with her schedule. I'm sure they'll do just fine."

"So humble, as usual," Mr. Lee said as he finished ringing her up.

"I'll tell my mama you said so. That'll make her happy."

"Here's your change, honey." His face had a sad look. Ash wondered what he was thinking. Was he worried about his kids, or about her? He always asked what she was up to, what she was learning. Sometimes she felt as though he might be sorry for her or upset. Like he thought that she wasn't normal.

Still, she smiled and waved at the grocer. "Thank you. I'll see you next week." She took the grocery bags and looked at the time. She'd been gone for over an hour. Mama hated when she was away for so long. She hurried home. The groceries in her arms were piled so high they blocked most of her view, and that was likely the reason she felt someone bump into her. She squealed as she fell to the ground.

The contents of her bags spilled out in a sprawling pattern in the lot. She saw a short man with a kind smile and small brown eyes looking back at her. "Oh, gosh, I'm so sorry, sir. So, so, so, sorry. I didn't see you." She was as sorry as she profusely expressed. Embarrassed as well. She shuffled to put her items back in order.

"It's quite arigh.' Not a problem." He reached down to collect the groceries. After handing the last apple to Ash, he straightened up, cleaning his Kiton suit with his short fingers. His expensive cufflinks bore the letter E. His brown tie matched his shoes and the color of his eyes. He fixed his hat and cleared his throat.

"Ok, sir. So sorry. Again." Ash gathered up her grocery bags. She wasn't used to interacting with many people, and even this small encounter made her nervous.

"Lemme help ya with those, they are quite heavy."

She shook her head. "Oh, no need, sir. I got it. I don't want to cause you any more problems."

"Ya don' want them to go flyin' out your hands again. Here, give me a bag or two," he insisted. The wrinkles around his eyes edged into their crease as he smiled.

"Thank you," she said, fearing she would insult the man if she kept declining his help.

"Not a problem, dear. Do ya live aroun' he'?"

"Yes, not too far away I've lived here all my life."

"Is'a nice neighborhood. I'm kinda new to these parts," he said.

"Oh? Where are you from?" The man seemed nice. Ash found that she liked his company. She was happy she had run into someone to talk to other than Mama or Mr. Lee.

"The city."

Ash smiled, then frowned. She only had TV and newspaper images as references to what the city looked like. "Oh, I haven't been there yet, but I want to go. My mama's pretty strict with me going outside the house so much."

"Well, a bit too overprotective, I say. Otha' people can take advantage of ya, but sometimes ya have to do what's best for yaself. Follow them dreams, or they will fade away."

Ash liked what the man said. "That makes sense. Yeah. And you're right. But to say Mama is overprotective is an understatement." She smiled and continued. "I was homeschooled, and home for everything. Still am. But Mama is great though, always watching me, making sure I'm safe and sound."

They walked a few feet from the store before she stopped. "Oop, here's my car," she said to the man as she located her keys. "Thank you, sir for helping. I'm so sorry to have bumped into you like that."

"Thank ya for knocking me off my feet," he replied, taking off his hat, exposing his shiny bald scalp.

Ash gave a sheepish laugh "Ok, then. Bye."

"One mo' thing." The man stopped for a moment. "If ya happen to know anybody who's lookin' to buy some real estate, please pass this along." He reached into his left pocket and pulled out a small stack of business cards. Ash placed the grocery bags in the back seat of the car before she read them. "Edward Bile-Real Estate Guru of Manhattan, Long Island, and Beyond" she read. "I don't think I know anyone, but if anything changes..." she waved the card "I will pass your contact along."

"Thanks for the favor in advance, lil' lady," the man said as he waved and turned to leave.

"Bye, and welcome to the neighborhood, Mr. Bile!"

⚜

The sun was still hot and bright when Ash arrived at the front doors of the mansion.

"Mama I'm back," she called.

"Good. What took so long, girl? Everything has been set up for hours."

"Hours? But I've only been gone for... oh, never mind." Ash hesitated "Please, not the lessons again."

"Darling, you must learn your mother's trade." She rearranged the candles on the glass living room table, then pushed the chair outward welcoming Ash to sit.

"But I don't want to learn this stuff." Ash noticed a bit of whining in her voice.

"Then what do you want, child?" Zilda snapped, tone sharp as a razor.

Ash was happy no matter how Zilda spoke to her. She hugged her mama, but Zilda didn't move a muscle to return the embrace.

"I want to go to the city. I want to work on stories, solve mysteries, and report on them on live TV. I want to be a journalist—you know that," she said cradling the idea in her mind. "And how am I to do that If you don't allow me to leave the Island?" She gave Zilda a soft smile.

Zilda replied with a stern look. Shrugging her shoulders, Ash walked over to the opposite side of the table, to an unwelcoming chair. "I know you're against letting me out of this home. I guess we should just start. I'm sorry I said anything." She plopped herself on the chair and let out a long, tired breath.

"Why do you have to be so difficult, darling? Any girl would dream of learning what I'm teaching you. Imagine all the power you will possess knowing how to manipulate this world, how to use magic."

"Mama, I don't want to manipulate. I just want a normal life, I want to go to a normal school, have friends, go to the beach, light a campfire. I want to investigate crime scenes. I want to bring bad people to justice." Ash looked down at the carpet. She knew she'd over-stepped. Said too much.

"Erase that from your head, child. And don't you ever, *ever* mention it again. Understood? You are to stay here with me," Zilda snapped, lighting one of the candles.

Although she knew she was overstepping again, Ash couldn't let the conversation die. "Please? You know I love you very much, but you do realize I can't stay here all my life. I'm not a child. I'm seventeen. I want a life outside of this mansion, outside of magic spell lessons. Can we at least come to some sort of agreement, maybe just about going to school for Journalism? At least the school, Mama? Please?"

"I taught you everything you'll need to know at such a young age. You are wiser than all the kids of New York City combined. What more do you want?"

Ash noticed the candles blew out as soon as Zilda turned to look at them. Without saying a word, Ash blinked her blue-green eyes and smiled. She felt her mama's gaze, steady and sharp, with a flick of soft-ness in her clear, almond-shaped eyes.

ZILDA

Zilda studied the creature. With each new day she came to realize the child's beauty and kindness. How stunning it was.

Afraid for the first time in her life, Zilda experienced another new combination of feelings: human hatred paired with love. It was as if her insides had turned to mush. She did not understand how this was possible and assumed that she must have been evolving. Somehow becoming more human. Impossible. Witches didn't just evolve into humans. Unless maybe they experienced human love? The underworld, Delirium would never forgive her.

Time was running out. She needed to teach Ash magic that did not belong in this world. That was one of the last pieces Zilda needed to take her.

Ash was far too young for Zilda's final plan. She needed a few more years, and then Zilda would be eternal at last—she could not bear these human feelings. They were more powerful than she had imagined. She had viewed Ash's mother as a weak creature. But now Zilda had felt human emotion and understood why Ash's mother trembled for her child. And there was power in it. Love. One that, if she had underestimated, perhaps Delirium had as well. She shook her head. *Silly thoughts, silly woman.*

Taking another look at Ash—*no, the Ortor*, Zilda reprimanded herself—a feeling of warmth, a summer's hug, squeezed somewhere to the left of her chest, she suspected it was what humans called a "heart." That muscle they had. Zilda did not believe she possessed this muscle, but sometimes it felt true. A real heart. A human heart that felt.

She turned away, ashamed. Shame was yet another feeling new for her. Every time she looked at Ash, she could not help but *want* to love. But Zilda did not want to want that. Perhaps she had been around the human for too long. That must have been the problem, and if it was, the solution would be as simple as sending the Ortor away for a time. That could break the chain of unwanted emotions Zilda experienced.

"You know what?" Zilda said, still looking away from Ash, trying to concentrate on the layer of dust by the fireplace. "I will make a deal with you."

It wouldn't hurt to promise the girl the stars, only to take her life when the time was right. Zilda pondered the arrangement and meaning of the words she wished to say. It seemed sensical to get the girl out of the house. Away from her. Absence made the heart forget. That was how she thought the human idiom went.

"Ok!" Ash replied. Her voice was chipper as usual.

"If you promise to devote your time and full energy to our lessons, you may enroll in school to study whatever it is you want to study."

Ash's eyes lit up. "Really? I can go to school? Even in the city?"

"Yes, yes, let's get on with it." She lit one candle with her eyes.

"Oh, thank you. You are the best. I love you so much!" Ash's dimples made her stunning smile even brighter. Zilda watched her jump up and down and clap her hands.

Somewhere deep within her form, where those "feeling" muscles and organs would be, Zilda felt satisfaction. And something that must have been joy for the Ortor. She hated it. Not good.

"Enough. Girl. Human love. Pathetic."

"I love you too, Mama," Ash replied as she often did. Assuming Zilda loved her.

"Never mind, child. Now, let us start with a warm-up" Zilda looked at the other candles and they lit back up. *Love.* What if she had said the same? But she would not because she denied the feeling, turning her attention back to the lesson.

"You have done this before, so let us do it again. This time with no flukes. Look at the candles Ash, concentrate. I want you to have the candles burn out in one instant, and then light up again. Just like I did, then turn the candles into liquid. Water, for now, will do."

Zilda watched the child. There was incredible progress from the last lesson. She suspected that Ash received her talent for magical art, from her great grandmother. That awful Ortor who killed so many of Zilda's kind.

"Good, darling. Very good. Now turn this water into blood"

"Blood?"

"Yes, I said blood."

The Ortor looked down. "But... but you told me that the blood we make with magic is blood we take from a person."

"Darling, do you think people get cuts, scrapes, get stabbed, or shot and bleed to death just like that? You cannot get something from nothing."

"But that means that I will make someone hurt." The Ortor carefully folded her hands on her lap.

"Darling Ash, it's just a small cup. Consider that someone nipped themselves a bit while cooking."

Ash exhaled. "I can't."

"I said do it. Or forget about school." Zilda felt anger, but she also felt pained for the girl. It was hard to dismiss.

"I won't even do it for school, no more using blood for magic. I don't want to be the person behind someone's pain, no matter how small."

"I said, do it, child. Or else I will ban you forever, disown you, and you shall be alone for the rest of your life," she said sternly.

"Don't get upset, please."

Zilda noticed how desperate Ash sounded, and it hurt *her*. "DO IT," she roared, hoping the anger would suppress the love, hide it deep down in an endless black hole.

"I'll do it, Mama, I will. Just don't get so upset it's not good for you."

"I'm the only person you have in this world child, and you dare to disobey me? You need to grow thicker skin."

Zilda watched as the Ortor concentrated, the way her eyebrows almost met at the apex of her nose. Within a few moments, the water turned light pink, then darker, red, and thicker.

"Good," Zilda said.

"There" Ash moved away from the table "There is your blood!"

"What's this? This..." Zilda picked up the cup, putting her finger in it, which she then licked. "This is ketchup. I told you. Blood, blood, blood!"

The Ortor's eyes dampened. "Mama, I'm tired."

"Leave me, you are good for nothing!" Zilda snapped, instantly feeling a knot of regret form in some empty cavity within her.

"I love you, Mama, I do."

CAGED BIRD II

ASH

I love you so much. I wish I had been with you. You deserve a family. And I failed to give you that, even though I was deprived as a child. Even though I could have done better.

You also deserve to know about your father.

— A LETTER

Ash was careful to slide off the chair. She tiptoed to the foyer. She grabbed a light sweater and stepped outside. The air was refreshing.

Even being on the porch felt liberating, Leaving the dust, dark, and suffocating walls of her home put her mind at ease. It was funny, in a sad way, that one's own home could turn into a prison.

The sun was setting, and the evening grew chilly. Ash enjoyed the breeze on her cheeks. She continued to wonder why her mama pressured her into magic. This was her life; a dusty home, no guests—not even pets, unless she counted the frogs, snakes, and spiders.

Mama and magic. Magic spells, magic frogs, magic snakes, and magic spiders. She felt sick to her stomach. She wasn't sure how long she could keep up with Mama's demands. She shivered against the breeze, and out of fear. Fear for her future, as she was incapable of escaping the shackles of her life. Fear of the world she might never know. But at the same time, she was confident that if given the chance, she would succeed in anything she put her mind to. She could investigate, report crimes.

She took baby steps down the stairs and headed onto the four-car driveway, reluctant to look away from the sky. Mama would be fine without her, she figured. The mansion was too big for only the two of them, anyway. The loud emptiness of the place was too much to stand.

The sky distracted her once again. The pink, yellow, and blue sunset was mesmerizing. All the colors intermixing at the same time. It prompted thoughts of promise. Hope.

She walked for a while and found herself about half a mile away from the mansion, by Tepenzee Park. A small road led the way to colorful trees; it was peaceful.

"Hello again." She heard a familiar but indistinguishable voice behind her. She tensed up a bit.

She turned around and relaxed her posture when she saw that, once again, she'd run into the man from the store. "Oh, Hi Edward. I mean, Mr. Bile."

"We seem to be bumpin' into each otha' lately," he said. Ash noticed movement at his stomach level. He was holding a pup in his hands.

"Oh gosh," Ash exclaimed clapping her hands. "This is a Cavalier King Charles Spaniel. So cute. What's its name?" She bent a bit to look at the pup before petting it.

"Wow, how ya know his breed? His name is Coco, I'm still potty trainin' him. It works well out here. He likes walks in the park."

"I wish I had a pet, but my mama can't stand animals for some reason."

"Sad ta hear that. How did ya know his breed?" Bile asked again.

"I guess from homeschooling, lots and lots and lots of books and Mama. She seems to know everything. Whenever I have one question, she gets really into it—sort of like an encyclopedia, I've learned a lot from her. She always says I have an extremely high intelligence quotient, just like her," Ash said letting out a deep breath.

"Ya don' sound too happy," Ed suggested. "He', why dontch'a hold him for a bit." He held Coco out for Ash to take. She did.

"Oh, he is so adorable," she gushed. "Hi, Coco." She smiled at the pup, and when she looked back at Ed, his expression held some sort of anticipation. Nothing as aggressive as an expectation, but Ash sensed a question waiting to be answered.

"I'm fine. Was just wondering about the world out there. You know. What it's like to be free." Ash took a stab at it. Their conversation in the parking lot came back to her. He seemed to think she should be free as well.

"Can I tell ya somethin'? I mean it sounds like ya feel imprisoned. I don' wanna impose, or anythin', just know ya ain't the only one. I mean to say it ain't easy. Ya see yo' share of worries out there, and it kinda gets to ya. Someone else's weight spills out onto every one of us, and sometimes ya can feel suffocated. So ya see, we are not tha' free, even when we thin' we are."

The breeze brought a calm wave to the sunset-glistened leaves surrounding them. Ash looked to her wristwatch for the time.

"Oh, my. I got to get going, Mr. Bile." She handed Coco back to him. "It's getting late. Mama will get worried."

"Course. I'll walk ya back."

"No, no it's fine. If Mama sees you... Let's just say she doesn't like guests too much."

"Don' worry about its kid, I jus' wanna make sure ya get home a'right in one piece. Okay?"

Ash agreed.

❧

They approached the Mansion. "Beautiful home ya got there Miss..."

"Ash. Ash Wise"

"Nice to formally meet ya, Ms. Wise."

"So nice to have met you again, and Coco. Hope to see you again Mr. Bile."

"You can call me Ed."

THE CAGE DOOR OPENS

ASH
Summer
1960s

Your father... was the kindest, most loving man. He often helped strangers. His love was limitless, and he gave it freely to those in need. He was the only light in my dark world until you came along, with your blue eyes and auburn hair. You look so like him already. I hope you can find his family. I hope that his children know how deeply loved they were, and that while I did take him away, he didn't choose to leave. His hand was forced. He never wanted me.

— A LETTER

"And the award from the American National Association of Journalism for top student in Investigative Journalism goes to the one and only Ash Wise." A roar of applause filled the large auditorium.

"Thank you." Ash beamed. She'd planned her outfit carefully. Her cherry lipstick complimented the light red locks hanging over her forehead. The diamond-shaped glass award sat on a bronze base and had more weight than Ash anticipated. It read "ANAJ excellence in Journalism Award." After receiving her award, Ash went down the steps to take a seat at one of the front chairs marked 'reserved.'

The moderator responded to Ash's thanks. "Thank you for being an astonishing student, journalist, and investigator. May you always uncover the truth, tell the truth, know the truth, and write the truth."

He addressed the crowd again. "And now for the top Honor Roll Student to graduate from the New York Institute," the moderator locked eyes with Ash, "Ash Wise. Not only is she the first woman to graduate with such high marks, but she has already received job offers from our most prestigious news stations. Ash Wise, please come on up here once again to receive your honorees' diploma."

The auditorium roared with cheers and applause once again.

Ash went right back up. "Thank you again." She stood at the podium speaking into the microphone. Her voice steady, sharp, and satisfying like a song, like the blanket of the sun.

When she spoke everyone stared, drinking up every syllable.

"We can ascend to the greatest heights," she started. "I'll admit, I struggled. Struggled to get to where I'm now. It took enormous effort. Many times, I thought I couldn't do it. That I was not worthy. That it was impossible. Impossible, not only because women are regarded differently than men in my field of study, in this line of work; but also because I experienced personal struggles. We all do. We must tell ourselves that we are unique, irreplaceable. Adapt to each challenge and welcome them as they come. Couple your arduous work with love, and you will get there. I had amazing mentors, teachers, and university staff who have helped me accomplish my goals. I'm looking forward to making positive change in our society by uncovering the truth and sharing it with the world."

More cheers followed. She slightly lifted her gown to climb down the stage. She knew she could not stay for the rest of the graduation ceremony. Mama hadn't attended. She hated crowds, and people in general. Ash had to hurry home to see her. After all, she owed most of her success to Mama. Mama taught her everything she knew. History, politics, mathematics, languages, arts. The only thing Ash didn't look forward to were her magic lessons. Even knowing they were coming; she would enter the house with a smile to greet Mama. Ash hated upsetting her and felt that something was off lately. Mama seemed more anxious than usual, but less irritated by Ash's complaints concerning the lessons.

Ash swung open the front door. Unable to contain her joy, she yelled down the hallway and up the stairs, "Mama. I'm home!"

"Not staying around with friends?" a slightly hoarse voice replied from the family room.

"You know I don't have time for friends, it's school and home for me."

"Good."

Ash noticed her mama's relief and even a slight smile. She felt Mama wanted to envelop her in a tight hug, or maybe even ask how the graduation went. But Mama sat on the couch next to the small table, candles lit.

"Now that you're back, we're ready to start practicing."

"I'm so tired from today's ceremony, and I still have an essay to submit. Do you want to hear how the graduation went?"

Zilda ignored her question "When we agreed to this Ash, you promised that your studies would not interfere with our practices."

"Yes, yes. Mama, I know." Ash sighed. She just wanted to make Mama happy. "So, what am I turning to blood now?"

"Today, we are turning water into fire, darling. This will help you in manipulating matter, nature, and eventually, minds. Once you learn to control and manipulate the natural order of the world, humans will be a piece of cake."

Ash sighed. She was tired of having to tell her mama what she wanted to do and what she didn't.

"But I don't want to manipulate anything or anyone."

"Hush your mind, child."

"I suppose. Let's get on with it, Mama."

"Now that's better."

Ash noticed how impressed Mama looked when the water turned to fire in a fraction of a minute. That pride from her mama was all she wanted in the world, but Ash wished Mama could find pride in the things she did for herself, and not just for her mama.

"You are doing so well, darling. You have so much power. You can use it on anything, anyone you want. You can cast a love spell, be the best journalist in the world, make it snow in summer, have food on your table without going to the store or working. You can hurt, steal, kill. You can do anything your heart desires." Zilda beamed.

Ash wanted to hear Mama acknowledge her real-world work. But she didn't want anything to do with magic. "I don't like using magic. You told me that using my powers takes away the good in this world. I don't want others to suffer on my behalf."

"You don't understand a thing." Zilda scoffed. The wrinkles that had started to show on her forehead creased deeper as she raised her eyebrows. "We are done here, clean up this mess now."

"I still love you, Mama." Ash smiled, hugged her, and whistled as she cleared the table.

"No whistling in the house. Else you will bring bad luck."

ZILDA

While Ash was cleaning the small table, Zilda studied the Ortor. Ash was almost ripe enough to use for Zilda's final plan. But the thought of killing the creature brought pain. A feeling Zilda hated as much as she hated the seeping feeling of love and care.

Zilda knew that if she did not take Ash's youth soon, she would fail her mission, and the underworld would go into hibernation until she started over and completed it. Delirium would not be pleased. The other witches would probably talk him into sending her off to the forest of the damned. Zilda could not stand eating muffins and drinking tea for breakfast. She wanted to be back in her world, with the demons and witches who feasted on maggots and dead bodies and thrived on death. But at the same time, Ash was holding her heart. The thumping organ was there. And it pumped red human blood throughout her perfect human form.

It was only a matter of months before she would have to take Ash's life, and she had to act fast. Otherwise, she would melt into a pool of motherly love, and die in it.

She felt a sudden weakness, and her whole body shook as she developed a cold sweat. She had started feeling the shivers, the cold perspiration months ago. She tried to control the pain, hide it from Ash, but she could hide it no longer. She knew too well that the shivers meant—the beginning of her end. Her own beauty and youth was leaving her.

There were wrinkles on her forehead and sunspots on her hands. Her bones had started to ache, and her eyes were losing their spark. Her platinum hair had thinned and taken a dry appearance. The funny part was, Zilda no longer cared about the imperfections, the tears, and breaks in her skin and body. If she was honest with herself, she did not care about the mission as much as she should have. This was her inner conflict. She had always possessed immense control before taking human form. But instead of being in control, she'd ended up allowing a mortal to influence her in an unacceptable manner. That was why it had been so hard to take anything from Ash. Instead, she gave her things. Hope, schooling that made her happy. She also knew that aging from drinking souls could take weeks, days, or even hours.

But she did not care, and she liked that feeling. The feeling. Love.

CHANGES

ASH

"At last, I wish this for you—that you grow to be nothing *like me. I wish for you to possess all of your father's best traits, and none of my worst. It's too late for me, dear. But it's never too late for you, so long as you live. I love you. I will love you forever."*

— A LETTER

Ash watched Zilda turn pallid, and she placed her hand on Zilda's forehead to check for fever.

"Mama, are you Ok? Mama, say something!"

"Yes darling. I am tired, that's all. I'm going to take a rest."

"You look as if you're about to faint, are you feeling ill?"

"Will be fine, child, it's old age catching up to me," she said, and Ash saw a faint smile cross Zilda's lips. Before this, she had rarely seen

Mama smile. Not like this. There had been small smiles, but not real ones. This one was real. So was Mama's smile when Ash had agreed to create a burning spell. The aftermath of the spell took out electricity and started fires in the surrounding towns. A handful of people were hurt by this. Ash had cried for a week, but Mama smiled then. And she was smiling now.

"Mama you're young and beautiful. I don't want to hear this nonsense about old age."

And then she saw it, Mama's hands. They had turned brittle and old within an instant, and her fingers were bony and cracked. Ash took another look as she covered Zilda's hands with her own. "Mama?" A wave of confusion spun in Ash's head. "What is this?"

Ash gradually took her hands off Zilda's, and she saw that her mama's hands were as normal as they had been before.

"Is this some sort of spell?"

"Leave me, child, I need rest. You shall know all in due time."

"Is this a new kind of magic, you haven't shown me yet?" Ash pressed, her inquisitive nature kicking in. She'd only really known magic as destructive. Mama never told her that she could heal others. Could she?

"I said leave this be," Zilda snapped.

Ash felt the shame in her mama's voice. "Mama. I'm sorry, I'm sure you'll tell me when the time is right."

"That is correct, child. For now, please help me get upstairs, I need rest."

Ash obeyed, hoping she would get to talk to Mama about what was happening, sooner rather than later.

❧

The weather in May on Long Island carried with it a fresh breeze of ocean air. The night was a little chilly but refreshing nonetheless. The trees started to show their colors and blooms. The brightly lit path led to their regular bench at Tepenzee park.

"Can you believe it?" It was the perfect end to a perfect day. Ash looked to the stars. She watched with a smile as Coco poked around in the grass.

"Course I can. I had never doubted ya." She noticed Ed give her a quizzical look.

"I'm so thankful we bumped into each other five years ago because it was you who helped me all along, you know?"

 "Me?" Ed asked.

"Sure. You always told me to follow my dreams. You told me to be strong and stand by what I want in life. 'Never think less of yourself or what you can accomplish' you told me that." She picked up Coco and patted his fur. "I still can't believe that they want me. Me. To be an Anchorwoman for *NY Publications*. The most famous news outlet Ed!' She picked up Coco and raised him up to her lips to give him a smooch.

"Success ain't no accident. Ya deserved it." She saw the happiness in his eyes but there was alarm in them, too. Like he wanted to tell her something but was holding back

"Thank you for always being there for me, Ed. You're like the father I never had."

Ed swayed uncomfortably on the bench.

"What?" Ash asked, noting his discomfort. She lowered Coco back on to the grass.

"Nothin' Angel, it's nothin'."

She checked her wristwatch.

"He' ya go lookin' at ya watch again," Ed said smacking his lips.

"I was so excited; I forgot the time. I have to tell Mama the good news. I'm sure it will brighten her day. I just wish she felt better. The past few years have been really hard for us." Ash looked down.

"I'll walk ya home, kiddo" Ed picked Coco up from the grass and scooped the pup into his arms. Ash gave Coco a gentle pat and walked home with a skip in her step.

❧

"Mama?" Ash closed the double doors behind her after waving goodbye to Ed and Coco. "Mama I'm back from my interview, and guess what?" She took off her shoes and proceeded to the kitchen. "Mama. Where are you?" She looked around the empty kitchen and the living room.

"I have great news for you!" She walked up the marble staircase to Zilda's bedroom.

She found Zilda motionless on her bed.

She ran to her mother. "Mama." She lightly shook Zilda's left shoulder.

"Yes, darling?" Zilda asked. Her voice was small and faint.

"Do you need anything? Maybe some water, medicine? Maybe we should finally call a doctor." Ash took another good look at Zilda. Her vivid beautiful Mama was withering away to an unfamiliar person. Not herself. Mama couldn't be so old...

"What is happening to you? You have to tell me, you promised to tell me. It's been years, and you are still hiding whatever it is. Maybe I can help you? I want to help you. I can't lose you, you're all I have." Ash held back tears.

❧

ZILDA

Zilda turned to look at the child. She knew all too well what she had to do to survive. Take the girl's life. But she could not. She could not do it. She had tried many times. Each time, she told herself she would wait for the next year. Next year, she'd kill the child. It was always next year, but she had never worked up the nerve to follow through. The girl had endeared her. Zilda loved the girl as if she was her own daughter. And Zilda was going to die for it.

"I thought," Zilda spoke, "that youth and eternity were the way of life. This was what I was told by those who come from my world. They were using me. I was to take the last Ortor from the earth. Eventually, this would enable us to take over all human souls."

"What are you talking about?" Ash's hand felt soothing on Zilda's deeply wrinkled forehead. She wanted the child to embrace her as she always did. She wanted to feel the warmth of her heart and see her smile.

"Mama, you're burning up. Let me try to summon a healing spell," Ash offered. And that brought another pain, that horrible love, to Zilda's heart. Zilda knew Ash hated using magic, knowing that the child offered it to help, melted her heart. The love was only so terrible because it could not last. She had to leave it on Earth.

"No!" Zilda raised her voice, signaling Ash to stop. "No magic. Your healing spell will not work on me, there are other things at stake. You must not try."

"But... why?"

"I cannot talk much now, darling. I also cannot explain every detail or why you wouldn't be able to heal me." She tried to take a deep breath. "But I will try to explain something else. Something very important." Zilda's lips curved into a smile when Ash sat on the side of her bed. Her daughter's presence calmed her. She was now at peace with the love that had consumed her. She wanted to give to Ash, she wanted to embrace her, she wanted to see her happy.

"Ok."

As hard as it was for Zilda to speak, she felt that she had to acknowledge the good news her child wanted to share. "Congratulations on your new job. You'll make a brilliant reporter."

"How did you know?" Ash tried to squeeze out a smile, but her lips twisted, and her eyes revealed concern.

"I know more than I've let on, darling, and for that, I apologize. But that aside, I wanted to give you a gift, so I asked your friend Ed to help me secure a cozy apartment for you in the city. If you wish, you can stay there. It will be easier for you to commute."

Ash's face lit up. "You bought me an apartment? Outside this mansion?"

"It's time you build your life, darling. You're free." A cough escaped her dry thin lips.

Ash leaned farther forward. "Shh. Mama, I won't leave you."

"You have to, darling. I gave you nothing in this life. But you, child, you gave me everything. You taught me love, you showed me how to feel. Pure love breaks evil." She couldn't recognize the old and croaky voice that formed her words.

Ash turned away, and Zilda knew the child did not want her to see the tears.

"I don't understand. You're ok. Probably just very tired. You should rest. I'll be right back." Ash moved to get up.

Zilda knew what was on the girl's mind. "Stop. You cannot cast that spell, darling. If you do, both of us will die."

Ash dismissed the warning and kissed Zilda on the forehead. "You need some rest. I'll be back in just a second."

"Wait. I must tell you something important," Zilda tried to reason, but Ash was out the door.

While Ash was downstairs going through the kitchen cabinet looking for items to put together a healing spell, Zilda heard the bedroom door close on its own. She felt the coldest chill. She steadied her voice.

The room fogged, then smoldered. The carpets and drapes glowed until they turned to fire, and the cause of the fire appeared before her.

"Delirium." Zilda gasped, staring at the elongated, fur-covered body of her master. His lifeless green-black eyes tore into her. He silently approached the bed. His extra-long barefoot legs resembled hooves, which dragged behind him. Before, this would not have startled Zilda. She would have been unafraid. Thrilled, even. But the human aspects of her drew in fear and a fight or flight response. She chose to ignore those instincts. They were not hers, after all.

"You haven't changed a bit," Zilda said with a fake smile.

Delirium waved his hand in front of her face as if he were about to hit her across her sagging cheek. His twenty-four fingers lit up with flames. He had four pointy ears, two on each side of his head, and his nose covered almost his entire face lengthwise. His head touched the ceiling, and a long thick, green tail circled his body like a giant snake. Delirium moved closer to Zilda, and the stench of rotten potatoes filled the air as he opened his big mouth to speak, exposing fifty fangs.

He almost roared with rage. "I will make sure you suffer, witch, for what you have done." His eyes reddened. His tail flicked back and forth.

"Delirium. You have come for a visit? Or shall I take my own life?"

Her third eye appeared and opened from beneath her skin. She felt a shooting pain above the bridge of her nose.

"How could you?" the unpleasant voice asked. "She was supposed to be yours years ago. You. The strongest spirit witch of our kind. The last one capable of occupying this world as your home, to pave the way for the rest of us. Perhaps I should have foreseen that the ease with which you traverse worlds was a strong indicator that the human world could influence you. That you would betray us all for human love. I mustered all the power I had to get up here, Zilda. You know what that means?"

Zilda laughed. "I know one thing. That you know nothing of love in this world."

The air grew colder as the flames raged on. "And I intend to keep it so. I sent you here to gain eternity and open the gates. We trusted you.

Feeling? How disgusting. You might as well have risen to the angels instead. How could you allow mortal love to infiltrate you? You have been contaminated. Just like the others."

"You try living in this world for two centuries, Delirium."

"How dare you speak to *me* like that?"

Zilda laughed carelessly.

"I will make sure you are banned from entering our realms. You are not even worthy to stay in the forest of the damned. You will die a painful slow death in the body of the old woman you hate so much."

"Do you think I care about our world anymore, or about looking old?" Zilda chuckled.

"Even if you change your mind and try to extract the soul from that Ortor, you will die."

"And you are not listening to me. Besides, what will you gain from my death? I'm the only spirit left to assure our survival," Zilda replied simply. As though the death of her kind was a normal occurrence that below-ground creatures had known.

"Our world will find another way to prosper. We will prevail," he continued, taking another step closer, piercing Zilda's almost lifeless eyes with his endless blackness. "There will be another witch born. And I can assure you that we will have this world while humans serve at our feet."

Zilda closed her eyes. "If you must kill me, do it."

"That would be too easy on you. You enjoy humanity so much, I believe you should suffer a human's death," came the reply. But Zilda knew. She could see the strain Delirium was under. Being in this realm was not simple for him. The physics were different. Everything was different. The demon was in pain. She understood that now. And she almost felt sorry for him. Almost.

Zilda hoped Ash could not hear his roars, hoped Ash would not return before he left. She did not have to worry for long. The chill lifted from the room, the flames dissipated, and Delirium was gone.

Zilda raised her fingers to the bridge of her nose and covered her third eye with the flap of skin, hoping it would blend out of visual existence before Ash returned to her side.

ASH

Ash looked through all the cabinets. She was missing white rose seeds to complete the healing spell. She had to go to the store to get some, but first, she mixed hot tea with turmeric and goat milk and went back upstairs to check on her mother.

"Mama. I made you the best brew of chamomile tea." She entered the bedroom, setting the tray with the tea on the nightstand. The air seemed much colder than before, and she shivered.

"Ohh, it's cold in here. Are the windows open?"

She couldn't believe her eyes when she looked at Mama. Zilda seemed to have aged terribly within just a few moments.

"Oh, Mama, you don't look good at all."

Zilda touched her face. "Ah, yes. I remember this feeling. Could you do me a favor? Hand me a mirror, darling."

Ash was surprised. Mama had avoided looking in the mirror for the past few years, but she did as Mama asked and handed her a small cosmetic mirror. She noticed how Mama brushed her bony fingers against her shriveled skin, as though trying to iron the wrinkles out. She couldn't recognize her. Only her eyes had a little bit of Mama left in them.

"Ash, I must tell you something very important." Zilda sat up.

"I'm listening." Ash noticed Zilda squint, trying to hide something. But Ash caught the meaning of what she saw in her mother's eyes. Panic, and regret.

"Your real name is Angela. I gave you the name Ash, but it does not belong to you, and you do not belong to me. Your real mother's name was Julia. She went by Julia Wise."

Ash felt a lump form in her throat. A wave of heat flushed all over her body. She wanted to scream for Mama to stop talking, but her tongue was leaden. She couldn't speak. Ash swallowed the lump back. She wanted to close her ears. She wanted to get up and run. But she could not move.

"I will tell you everything, but you must promise to listen and not interrupt as there is very little time left for me in this world."

Zilda relayed much of what seemed to be a true story to Ash. In just a few moments, Ash learned that her parents were no longer alive and hadn't been for some time, that she was taken away by Zilda, and that there was a war between the witches and the Ortors.

"You are the most powerful Ortor I have ever seen. The way you caught on when we studied magic. Unbelievable."

"You... how could you do that to my parents? To me? You lied to me. You lied about everything!" Ash demanded more information. She felt numb all over. Her lips moved but nothing came out. Time slowed to a crawl, but the motion of the room kept up with it regardless. Mama was trying to say something, but Ash couldn't hear, she just saw her lips move slow and steady. She noticed a sunbird land on a branch outside the window and how it flapped its wings, and everything was in high focus and slow. She noticed the blue and red pattern on the bird's belly and saw how it opened its beak to sing a short song, then it spread its wings and flew away. Away from Zilda. And then everything went back to the way it was before; the room and Zilda's words seemed real again. Ash never cried much, but this time she couldn't help it, she felt a tear roll down her face.

Zilda took a deep breath. "I'm sorry Ash. It was my duty to do what I did, but you showed me another side of life. I can feel. There is nothing I can do to take away the pain you are experiencing. I can't bring your parents back. Please forgive me."

For the first time in her life, Ash saw tears stream down Zilda's face. Large, wet tears.

Now everything was moving fast, like a time capsule swishing quickly but, almost unnoticeable. Words flew like daggers, sharp, and jabbing. Ash couldn't think. She took a step back.

"Forgive? For lying to me? For calling me your daughter? For my parents' fate? For treating me like an unneeded dirty pet?"

"Ash, please try to understand. I had to do it. I am not from this world, and it was my nature. I had a chance to take your life years ago, but I couldn't do it. I love you as a mother loves her own child. I can't understand how, but your innocence, your love, has won me over, and now I'm paying for it with my life."

"Life? How dare *you* speak about life?"

Ash couldn't stand that Zilda ignored her outburst. Instead, she noticed her open the nightstand and reach into the drawer. A mesmerizing, pear-shaped, sapphire diamond ring shone like a star from Zilda's palm. She also took out a chain with a locket, the letter J inscribed on its face.

"This ring was your mother's. Your father gave it to her. This locket. It belonged to her, a gift from her parents. They gifted this to her on her seventh birthday. Hoping the message inside would help her defeat me."

"My father. Who was he? What was his name?" More words, more questions, more daggers.

"He's gone. Everything I did was so that I could keep you."

"You lie. Tell me the truth, I deserve to know. Tell me now." She wanted to swing her fists, she wanted to punch something, she wanted to yell until the world heard. But she could not move, her head told her to act, but her body wouldn't listen.

"If your mother would have listened to me—"

"Who was my father?" Ash yelled. She instinctively ran toward Zilda, as if she would slap the woman. This stranger. Not her mama. Her mama was someone else.

Zilda's eyes rolled back until Ash saw only the yellowing whites, shutting down like an iron gate, and she saw how Zilda fought to open them.

"Tell me. Tell me everything you know." Ash was surprised by the edge in her own voice.

"I must warn you not to practice magic anymore. Forget everything I taught you about its existence. I should have stopped long ago. Long, long ago." She sighed, and the inhalation rattled. "If you use magic, a demon, Delirium, will resurrect. It will awaken dark forces from my world. Do you understand? I'm sorry. I love you, Ash."

Ash knew there was more left unsaid. She tried to get that information. She tried to keep Zilda awake. But it was useless.

Her fingers curled into fists. "Do not call me Ash. My name is Angela. Angela Wise." She wasn't sure if she wanted to cry for Zilda, for what she'd just learned, or for both. She noticed how Zilda's body withered, and it did not surprise her. Nothing surprised her anymore. After all, there was another world, she was an Ortor, and she had a secret past. Zilda's skin turned to grey, her beautiful hair was no more. An ugly, small being lay motionless on the polished wood bed surrounded by pretty white and gold-laced pillows.

Angela felt a shiver and the piercing cold. She noticed a plume of white exit Zilda's body. The almost transparent cloud was shaped like a human, and then another human-shaped cloud puffed up, and another, and another. Hundreds of them rose from Zilda's core, shooting up in the air like fireworks.

"Dead souls," Angela whispered at the mist, still glued to the floor. Unable to move, she watched and shivered.

Twenty minutes passed before the last of the souls left Zilda's body, and as soon as they did, the body turned to dust and disappeared. Leaving the bed vacant and pretty again. The silk bedding, the laced white and gold pillows, the polished wood. Perfect and pretty.

Angela was left alone. Alone, and scared.

BREAKTHROUGH

ANGELA
Fall
Early 1970s

"Angela? What happened?" Liam wrapped her in his arms. "Your face… you look like a different person. Like you've seen a ghost. Are you ok?"

"I remember. I remember everything. And it's scary." She pulled back and covered her face with her palms.

"It's not everything I imagined. I'm more confused now than before. I should have never wished for my memories to return to me."

"That was something I was afraid of. Angela I'm sorry." Liam reached out to her.

"Zilda was not my real mother. I don't know my father's name. I have so many questions about my past. Even more than I had before I remembered. And I'm pissed. So, if you're still in the mood to bash this wall in, I'm ready. Let's do it, like right now."

"You have to calm down. Let's calm down before we do anything." Liam gave her another bear hug. "We will find everything you need to know. I promise. You have me, and you have your skills. You can dig through anything and find anything. You'll get your answers, Angela, it will be a piece of cake."

Angela took a deep breath. Liam shuffled his feet. Keeping his eyes down he said, "This is probably not the best time, but you deserve to know. I've... I've wanted to tell you for a while now. You know how you said that you don't know your own father's name?" He didn't let Angela answer before he continued.

"Well, I know *my* father's name, and I remember how excited we all were when he came from work, handing each one of us a large bar of chocolate. I remember he and Mom were very much in love. We were happy, the five of us. And then he just disappeared. I was very young then."

"I'm so sorry." Angela let out a small breath. She felt terrible for him. And that was a gift and that was a curse because she now knew the sting of loss and abandonment, but she knew sympathy, too.

He continued. "And when I first met you and found out that you were working on a certain case, I figured I needed to be there with you. This case is more important to me than to anybody because... Jack Roe is my father."

Angela gasped.

"I'm sorry I didn't tell you earlier, but you were going through so much. And I truly love you, Angela. I love you like a sister, and I did not know if you would agree to take me along knowing that Jack Roe is my father. And I couldn't even offer you much information about him, because Mother *never* talks about him. All I know is his name, and that he was always smiling, and that he loved us all, but he vanished. And I need your help to figure this out."

Angela shook her head. She understood, but she was angry. "I guess I'll try to still be understanding. But it's hard because you've just admitted that I'm part of some agenda, and that's what I've always been. Part of someone's agenda. Never my own," she said. The bitterness was sharp in tone and feeling.

"Angela, I never intended on using you. I didn't know you were working on that case when we met. I didn't intend to use you for anything, not even when I saw those papers on Jack Roe. Not telling you was a way of coping with this pain, and I wasn't sure if telling you would change much anyway."

Angela shrugged and sighed. "I'm sorry about your father, Liam. I'll do anything I can to crack this case. Mostly because it's my job and you can help me with it, but also because even though I feel like dirt right now, I still want to help you."

Liam's shoulders slumped. His head was down, and he barely met her eyes. "This was the only piece of information I kept from you. You know everything about me now. My family doesn't even know what you know."

Angela inhaled, trying to keep her heart steady. All this information was making her dizzy again. She realized that she'd just attended a party and mingled with the very family that could have given her some answers on the case.

"My mother and siblings have no idea I sway the other way. You know I can't tell a soul. I will probably get disowned, my business destroyed, and God knows what else. I had to deal with these feelings of being trapped. And deal with my mother asking me when I'll get hitched. I had to explain to Mother and Caiden so many times that you were just a friend. Especially Caiden."

He started pacing from one end of the room to the other.

"Can you stop that? The pacing?"

"Sorry. Yeah. I just... I want answers. Like you did, and I wanted to help you. Will you please still help me?"

Angela nodded. "Yeah. You did help me, you saved me. I owe you more than just answers, I owe you my life. We will figure it out, Liam. Together."

"Ready to break this thing down, once and for all?" he asked, taking the hammer in his hand.

"Never been so ready." Angela followed him to the hollow wall.

The wall was demolished in about two hours. They found themselves standing on top of a long staircase looking down into a dark cellar.

"I knew it," Liam exclaimed.

Angela took the first step, Liam followed. It was dark, and the smell of mold hit the air.

"There's a flashlight in the kitchen cabinet, can you get it?" Angela asked.

"I've already got one in my pocket." Liam handed her one flashlight and flicked on another that was in his hand.

To the right, they noticed a wine cellar holding exquisite, aged wine. The walls were lined with rare artwork. Everything was covered in layers of dust and spider webs. Liam couldn't take his eyes off the paintings.

"What are we looking for?" Angela was almost certain that he'd mentioned some hiding place for something important.

"Cellar equals safe, safe can equal money or secrets," Liam whispered as though he were a child telling a scary story in a tent. Angela liked the way he tried to make even serious things light-hearted.

"I don't see a safe anywhere, Liam. And why do you think this entrance would be sealed in the first place?" She was wondering out loud more than she was searching for an answer from her flashlight-bearing friend, but she got one anyway.

"I'm not sure, but look at these paintings Angela, it's as if they are trying to tell us something."

"What do you mean?"

"Look at the *Girl with a Pearl Earring*. The portrait is staring straight at the *Woman in Blue Reading a Letter* on the opposite wall. I think there might be something behind this painting." He walked over to Johannes Vermeer's *Woman in Blue Reading a Letter* and lifted it with extreme care to expose an enormous safe.

"Aha!" Liam exclaimed.

"Wow. How did you know?" Angela was amazed.

"There's a reason why I'm in this business," he said, not hiding the hint of pride in this voice. Angela smiled at his endearing characteristics again. He never would hide that hubris completely. He just couldn't.

"Where's the paper you found? With the numbers?"

He shook his head. "Don't need the paper. I remember those numbers by heart. 6982."

She paused. Her fingers hovered over the safe. It was as though she needed permission. She looked to Liam.

"Well. Go on." Liam backed away to the staircase and retreated up the stairs. Angela let out a faint "pfft" at his absconding before she turned back to the safe.

She repeated the numbers out loud. She was nervous and attempted to steady her hands. She continued to repeat the number over and over, and before she could even turn the full combination, the lock triggered, and there was a loud *click,* before the safe door swung open. She cursed herself for doing it again—for using magic without wanting to. She stood in silence before reaching into the safe.

Angela's small hands trembled as she felt around inside the safe. She removed a few items and laid them on the floor. She illuminated the contents and found a slew of jewelry—mostly diamonds with some pearls scattered in—and an awe-inducing amount of money.

When she'd sorted through the familiar feel of money, she reached back into the safe and pulled out a small box. Inside she found a sealed envelope.

To my dearest Angela, from your Mother Julia was written on the front face of the envelope.

"Liam, this is from my biological mother," Angela whispered to just the air, before she unfolded the letter. The page shook in her hands, but she began to read the wavering letters.

My dearest daughter, if you are reading this, you are unharmed. I procured the safe in which this letter rests, hoping to someday pass its contents onto my children. I only had a single daughter, and so that means that everything herein is yours. It belongs solely to you.

I want you to know that, even if it seemed otherwise—I've always loved you. I've loved you every second of every day. I have done some terrible things, but through all of my actions, I always held the image of your innocent eyes in my mind and in my heart.

This letter exists so that you can have access to knowledge—knowledge I didn't hold until it was too late. You come from a family with a unique lineage. You are what is known as an Ortor. Surely, by now, you've encountered things that cannot be explained by either sense or science. Those things are due to your bloodline, which possesses magical abilities to leverage against great evils. Ortors are often volatile beings because they do not understand their own powers, which leaves them vulnerable to the evil they should know to fight against. Dark witches will hunt you down in an otherwise normal world. Please be careful. You were likely left in the dark about all of this, and if I do one thing right in my life it is this: I will not allow you to suffer the fate that I did.

My mother—your grandmother—nearly saved me from the clutches of a dark witch who went by the name of Zilda. Because my mother could not fully save me, I was doomed to a life of begging on the streets without knowledge of most of my past life. Typically, dark witches are easy to detect. You'd know not to follow such a witch simply because they offer you lavish things, or what your heart most desires. I did not know this. I was innocent, young, and homeless. I followed Zilda.

Witches like Zilda feed on the newest generations of Ortors, and we often do not make it through their clutches. They look for the daughters, like you. While my mother saved me, she did not eliminate Zilda from this world. Eventually, Zilda offered me a life I desperately wished to have. I was so foolish. I hope you'll forgive me for the words I will write next.

What I wanted, more than anything, was a life with your father. And Zilda gave me that. Your father was mine. But his love—it was not real. That love was produced by a spell. Child, at first, I did not mind. That's the biggest sin I must confess. Though you may find my confessions afterward to be dreadful, still, they hold no candle to the original sin, which was acceptance of an unrequited love. That unrequited love was all I had. There was no memory of my life before the streets of Manhattan. I had nothing, child.

Your father, however, had another family. It was as though that part of his life was a blank spot. Though he would go missing for several days, I thought nothing of it, as his work called him often to travel. That was my second sin—not questioning my life. Of course there would be terrible repercussions to the spell I so happily accepted.

We were cursed. Doomed to be miserable together. Mostly because I was aware that he never truly loved me. Not many had, other than my parents, and I could not remember them. I knew no true love of my own. Until I had you.

One thing I did know; you would be taken from me. And there would be little I could do to stop it. Please forgive me. There was an unknown clock ticking away, somewhere, the seconds with which I would spend with you. If I could find that device, I would destroy it with all my might.

I wish I knew what would become of you, or me.

That witch will continue to haunt us because she seeks access to eternity, and we are the channel through which her iniquitous ship can sail to reach it.

Zilda promised me that she would take your life when you reached seven years of age. But if you're reading this, you're either a very precocious youngster, or you've managed to escape your fate. I always had faith that you could do so. I knew that you were stronger than me. Better than me.

The only way to stop the witch is to defeat her. Forever. And I can offer no guidance for you as to how to do so. I apologize for this as well. But truly, I believe you are stronger than I ever was, brighter, kinder. "Pure love breaks evil." These are the only words my parents left for me.

Never practice magic if you haven't already. It poses a grave danger to you and to everyone. Do not use your Ortor powers. If you do, it will ignite that pure evil to ascend from below and ensconce the earth in its rot.

I love you so much. I wish I had been with you. You deserve a family. And I failed to give you that, even though I was deprived as a child. Even though I could have done better.

You also deserve to know about your father.

After she devoured the first page, she placed the letter back in the safe. She needed a moment. A deep breath. When she gained the courage to look at the final portion of the letter, she read that quickly, too.

Your father, Jack Roe, was the kindest, most loving man. He often helped strangers. His love was unlimited, and he gave it freely to those in need. He was the only light in my dark world until you came along, with your blue eyes and auburn hair. You look so like him already. I hope you can find his family. I hope that his children know how deeply loved they were, and that while I did take him away, he didn't choose to leave. His hand was forced. He never wanted me.

Zilda murdered your father. His body lies at Treasure Lake Cove. He deserved a proper burial. Where his family and children could grieve and say goodbye. He deserved that. So did they.

At last, I wish this for you—that you grow to be nothing *like me. I wish for you to possess all of your father's best traits, and none of my worst. It's too late for me, dear. But it's never too late for you, so long as you live. I love you. I will love you forever.*

THE NEW MRS. ROE

JULIA
Spring
1940s

"You know what I think?" Julia asked, as Jack traced the number eight on her bare back with his fingers.

"Mmm?"

"Not all fairy tales come with happy endings."

"Ours is happy."

Julia sat up to fluff her pillow. "You have kids, Jack. And a history with your ex-wife. And with me? What do you have with me?"

"With you I have... *you*. I have us, excitement. I have a new will to live. I have... love." She noticed he took a moment to think, the bland look returned to his face. Was that the spell wavering from him?

"The only thing I wanted my whole life was to figure out who I was, to maybe even find my parents one day. And you. I wanted you. But your kids. Jack, I cannot accept them. Your wife is not a problem, but your kids will not allow us to have a happy ending. They'll always be there, reminding you of your past."

And I'm not willing to share you with them, she wanted to say but bit her tongue.

He took a deep breath. "This is not easy on me, love. But I cannot and will not abandon my kids."

"Kids," Julia repeated. She played with the tassels of the toss pillow she'd sat in her lap. What was that pillow? Just dressing. No one used it, not really. It was just for looks. Appearances. She felt the sting of regret as she twisted the strands. She wanted to tear the whole thing apart.

"Two boys and a girl. And we will make it work, the five of us. I'm not going to let you go, nor will I let them go."

"How old are they?" she asked. "Won't let them go," she added, anger squeezing her heart until it hurt.

"Are you sure you're ready to know more about them?"

"No. I'm not." She looked up at him after she spoke this truth.

His eyes flashed with something she saw as a reflection of her own regret. He was unhappy with her answer. But he would never admit to it. "I don't blame you. Whenever you're ready, I'll tell you more about them. And one day, you'll get to meet them."

Julia scoffed, but she was remorseful. Jack's eyes met hers and she saw how his blank look changed into warm affectionate adoration. This is what she wanted from him, the Jack who was head over heels for her and only her.

"I have no idea what came over me, you are just spell binding. I want you. And I choose you." He hugged her tightly and pressed his lips against hers.

A small part of her wanted to scream at him. Tell him to leave, to go home to his family. She wanted to tell him everything about the witch, about the spell.

"You know what else I think?" she asked, pulling away.

"Mmm?"

"That true love can indeed be false."

"My! Julia, you say things that make me want to shelter you forever."
He plopped himself on the pillow, putting his palms behind his head.
"I'll tell you what true love is. It's the way I feel about you. An infinite
number of words could not come close to describing my love for you."
He licked his full lips and gave her one of his heroic smiles. "I'll try
anyway. Look, before I met you my world was black and white. But the
moment you arrived, color flowed in, light and color. And now it's all
bright, and everything is beautiful. Vibrant."

She gave him a sheepish smile, but she knew her own misery dragged it
down. Jack would not notice that. He scarcely noticed when she was
doubtful of his love, or if he did notice, he brushed it aside easily. It
was almost dismissible to her as well. Though his actions and words
screamed that he loved her—she knew that he never truly would. He
would never love her in any meaningful sense of the word. He would
love his children, though. The thought of his children ate at her. She
had to think of a way to make him leave them for good. Her heart
knotted, a lump in her throat formed, and she realized how miserable
she was, despite her happiness that she was with Jack. Maybe this was
the curse the old witch spoke of—the curse of never being truly happy.

Because she carried the burden of the truth, and the terrible feelings
that accompanied it.

Summer

The sun shone gently through the French stained-glass kitchen
windows. Being married to the man of her dreams thrilled Julia in a
way she could have never imagine, but at times, when Jack was away
for work, or with his children, she stayed in bed until the afternoon.
She dreaded meeting the three brats. When she and Jack were

together, they spent most of their mornings by the kitchen bar, next to the open window, sipping tea and talking. She never got tired of Jack telling her how much he was in love with her. Yet, she wasn't sure if she was more in love with him, her lifestyle, or both. She was grateful that she'd not had to deal with Jack's ex-wife, but she also wished that Jack wouldn't need to see his children. She had to do something to keep from sharing him with anyone.

She found him reading the morning paper. "Good morning," she said as she poured coffee into his favorite mug.

"Hey, you." He was combing his hands through his messy red curls. It reminded her of last night, how she ran her fingers through his curls when they made love. He was still wearing his dark navy robe, which was begging to be un-tied. She wanted to run her fingers alongside the muscles of his stomach. She poured cream into his mug and gave him a smirk, which he didn't notice because he was too busy reading the newspaper.

"Where's Veronica? Why isn't she making breakfast?" he asked. He took a sip of his coffee, eyes still on the paper.

"I told her not to come on Sundays anymore. I want Sunday to be our alone time, and the house is clean We don't need a maid seven days a week." She walked over to untie the robe, as she pressed her lips to his.

"Ohhh la, la, Mrs. Roe." He faked a French accent.

"So far, being Mrs. Roe has been amazing. Can you believe it? One whole year." She planted kisses on his neck.

"I like what you do to me," he purred.

She sat on his thighs facing him, slightly rocking her body.

"You have to stop visiting them, Jack," she whispered.

"Visiting who?" He still held the paper in his right hand and grabbed her waist with his left. He glared at her.

"Your old family, of course."

"They are my children, Julia. How can you say I have to stop visiting them?"

"Simple. I don't want them in our lives." She lifted herself off his lap and walked over to the fridge to slam its door.

"Do you want my children to think they don't have a father?" he asked, pretending to read the daily again.

Frankly, she did not care what his children thought. "They have their mother with them, they don't need you." She was furious that he didn't agree. He did not have the right to be ok with taking time away from her.

"Maybe, if you hadn't grown up as an orphan you would understand that children need both their parents," Jack snapped, throwing the daily on the floor. He tended to get his mind back when he thought of his children, and she hated that. His razor-sharp focus landed elsewhere.

She stomped her foot.

"I'm sorry, love." He stood and took a step closer to her, reaching with his perfect fingers to touch hers.

"Don't start, Jack."

"Just tell me, why is it that you have to poke and probe about my children almost daily?" He pulled her close to him "Let's just enjoy us."

"We are not discussing the whys right now. I'm telling you I don't want your children in your life, in *ours*." She pulled away from him and mixed sugar into her coffee before she slammed the mug down onto the table.

"Love. We are happy, everything is beyond amazing with us. Let us not rock the boat."

Julia walked over to the double doors overlooking the garden from their kitchen and stared into the light sky.

"What has gotten into you, love?"

Time got into her. Every single day she found herself boiling with jealousy and hatred for those brats.

"I don't recognize you. Whatever happened to my sweet wife, who was always full of life and smiles?" Jack asked as he slid himself into one of the bar stools.

"I just don't want anything to ruin us." She went back to the table and sat next to him. She understood that their marriage and her new life was a product of a supernatural power, and it ate her alive. He did not love her out of choice, but how she wanted him to absolutely love her, just her...

"It will be fine, love. I will not let anything happen to us. Seeing my children will not ruin our marriage. You should meet them one day. They will win your heart over." A flash of pure joy lit up his eyes.

"You see what happens to you when you even mention them?"

"What?"

"You get this... *thing* in your eyes. This spark that you never show me."

"You are being unreasonable right now. My children are innocent, happy little people, whom you will absolutely adore, I promise."

Julia's insides churned upon hearing him say such things, and she was sure that her eyes gleamed with hatred. "I'm going to take a shower," she said. Her tone was sharp as a blade and, she hoped, just as cutting.

The drops of soothing water melted away her rage. She looked at her engagement ring, twisting it side to side, admiring its beauty. Jack was such a good husband, but she wanted all of him.

She still had the same fears and questions. About Jack, about her parents. She knew the witch had answers, but Julia had given up on finding her.

As jealousy turned into anger, it began to consume Julia's life. All sorts of evil thoughts swam inside her clouded mind. Dark thoughts. Horrible things. Things that were not like her.

Killing his children had crossed her mind. When had she become so malevolent?

The shower gave her a sense of serenity. She stood another moment under the transparent drops before turning off the water. And that was when she had an idea that did not involve violence. She discovered another way for them to live undisturbed, and in peace together.

The weekend passed faster than usual. She checked the clock nearly every five minutes until it was almost time to set places for dinner.

She phoned Jack at work to ensure that he would be home after his meeting—about two hours ahead. After she had his reassurance and she hung up, she called the housemaid to her.

She greeted the woman. "Veronica."

"Yes, Ma'am." Veronica charged to Julia, sharp and prompt as usual, waiting to take orders.

"I'll be in the cellar, please let me know when you are ready to make dinner. I would like to help you this time."

"Help me?" Veronica asked. Julia saw her eyebrow twitch, as if the servant would dare raise it at her. But Veronica maintained her calm tone, though her hands shook. "Um. Of course, Ma'am Julia," she said sheepishly, running her palms down her apron to wipe off the sweat.

"You can go now, Veronica and do something with that hair and bonnet on your head. It is far too short. Doesn't suit your chunky face. Go on now. Shoo"

Veronica dashed to the kitchen.

On her way down to the cellar, Julia caught a glimpse of herself in the mirror. She couldn't help but think how much she'd changed in the last few years. Her expensive appearance did not surprise her anymore. Her long locks shined like dark rubies. Her pencil skirt fit perfectly against her flawless body. And of course, her jewelry. Always excessive and stunning. A new piece for a new day to match an outfit. She had enough jewels to stock a bank vault. Smiling at herself, she finally broke away from the mirror.

Although the cellar housed hundreds of exquisite wines, Jack found no need to visit. So, Julia chose the place to hide her most cherished possessions and her memories.

She stood in front of *The Woman in Blue Reading a Letter*. It had become one of her favorites. Looking back, Julia would never have imagined herself knowing so much about art, let alone owning it. She found herself visiting museums and taken aback by the stories artists represented. Perhaps it was the middle-class life portrait in Vermeer's work that drew her glance. Regardless, the contents behind the painting were more important to her than any work she owned.

She looked around the room. *The Girl with a Pearl Earring* stared back at her from the opposite wall. The Arnolfini Portrait sat next to *The Woman in Blue Reading a Letter*. Julia studied the painting by Jan van Eyck for the hundredth time. She loved its details. At one point, Julia even felt as innocent as the pregnant girl in the green gown.

"Ma'am Julia," she heard Veronica call from upstairs.

Enraged at the interruption by the stupid girl, Julia snapped. "I'll be right there, go back to the kitchen."

No more time to waste, Julia thought. This was it. She had to do what was best for herself and follow through with her plan. She found herself face to face with *The Woman in Blue Reading a Letter* and gave it a gentle nudge. The painting opened as if a door. Behind it, a safe securely nestled in the wall. Julia turned the dial of the lock. 6,9,8,2. It opened as well.

This safe was Jack's idea, a spot for safekeeping things they would acquire in the future. He had started a little nest egg in there but had quickly become too busy to maintain it. He had granted Julia access. Of course, she changed the combination and continued to add to the collection of what was inside. She enjoyed the control, the status, and the security.

"Ma'am Julia, I'm so sorry to bother you again, but you asked me to call you when I was ready to make dinner." Veronica was standing at the top of the stairs. Her nervousness was detectable in every shaky syllable.

"I said I'll be right there. Go back to the kitchen, girl. What? you can't understand English? Were you raised on the streets not to listen to what you are told by your superiors?" Julia yelled.

Veronica's eyes filled with tears before she looked down and dashed back to the kitchen. Julia should have felt some hint of guilt. Veronica was such a young girl. She worked for them to help her sick father, but since Jack showed her empathy and compassion, Julia felt free to treat her as she wished.

Julia could have sworn that she still felt the dumb girl's presence, but she shook the feeling away and continued her mission. She moved the fancy jewelry boxes and the stacks of cash around in the safe. She reached to the back and managed to remove a transparent tube. She wrapped her fingers around it and noted how small it was. So small it amazed her. It could put an end to her misery if she just added a drop of its contents to his meal.

She loved him, but she had to get rid herself of him. She could not bring herself to harm his children, and if Jack was gone, so too would go the horrid, cursed, painful jealousy and hatred that lurked in her heart. She unbuttoned the first three buttons of her silk blouse to house the tube safely between her breasts and closed to door to the vault, then she went right to the kitchen.

"You've started dinner, Veronica?"

Veronica jumped up. "Yes Ma'am Julia," she managed to reply.

"But I told you not to start without me, dear." Julia smiled through clenched teeth.

"I'm sorry, it's just that Sir Jack will be home soon, and you asked to have dinner ready on time." Veronica wiped her palms on her apron. Her plump cheeks turned red as overripe tomatoes; her eyes began to tear up again.

Julia smiled searching the cabinet for sugar. "No worries."

While Veronica busied herself with the eggs, Julia disposed of the sugar. "Doesn't the Caribbean Cornbread call for sugar?" Julia asked.

"Yes, of course"

"Well, I can't disappoint my husband dear, by not making his favorite dish. Why don't you run to the store and grab some sugar? I'll prepare the rest."

"I believe I saw sugar up in the..."

"Well, you saw wrong. Now go."

Julia brushed her hand between her breasts to ensure the small tube was safely in place. Veronica didn't move, her eyes locked in on Julia's hands.

"Well, what are you looking at, dear? Go on, your famous cornbread won't cook itself."

As soon as Veronica stepped out the door, Julia measured the flour and poured it into the egg mixture. She then took the tube out. Recalling how difficult it had been for her to find actual poison on the black market, she smirked. She enjoyed how much more articulate money seemed in those seedy situations than humans could ever be. Wealth was far more persuasive She had been able to find a chemist, even, who told her that once that particular poison hits the bloodstream, the target would be dead within one hour. The advantage of this poison was that no one would be able to pinpoint the cause of death.

She took another look at the tiny tube. Her plan was perfect. With Veronica in the house, she felt secure that no one would look her way. Veronica would be a witness to their lovely dinner, and then she would be witness to a sudden, but non-suspicious death. Perhaps a heart attack, or some other natural cause.

If Jack couldn't love Julia truly and fully, then he deserved death.

Cold and cruel. Her heart raced. She turned to the wine rack and picked up a bottle of Chateau Lafite, sipping it straight from the bottle She gulped it down like hungry lungs would take in air after a long run. She sank into the couch in her alcohol-fueled reverie.

VERONICA

Veronica was on her way to the supermarket. Not a far walk. She needed it, she needed to get away from that fathead. She hated Julia with her whole heart. Bitch always treated her like a rag. Mr. Jack wasn't that way. He was kind and nice, but Julia was pure evil. A stuck up, rich bitch. Veronica had no choice but to follow every one of Julia's whims. Her father was too sick. She couldn't lose her job. She had no idea how to make money fast, to afford the medication, to afford help for her father. Veronica was always a respectable person. She went to church. God forbid she took anything that didn't belong to her or told a lie. She liked to follow the book. Straight. Line by line.

No, she didn't know how to turn a quick buck. But she felt she was done with it, with the job, with the abuse. She was full of Julia's ugly words. Full to the neck. Stressed to the brim. God would forgive her. He would understand. That she sneaked up on bitch when bitch was in the cellar. She gave herself a pat on the back for being able to stand on top of those stairs so quiet and steady, seeing the whole thing. The money, the jewels, the little vial. In a way she was proud of herself, the way she was able to jot down the numbers 6982. Her hands got sweaty at the thought of what her apron pocket housed.

When she was done buying the sugar, she started her way back to the mansion. When she walked back, she called to the bitch. Whom she found, passed out cold on the couch. So cold, Veronica was certain she was dead.

"Ma'am Julia?" The next she knew, Veronica was begging her to wake up, asking her why she had killed herself while poking her. "Ma'am Julia! Please wake up!" One last plea before Julia became irritated and fully woke.

"Stop. Please, stop calling me Ma'am, Veronica. Just call me Julia." Julia opened one eye, and gestured for Veronica to move out of the way. The scent of wine lingered on the woman's breath.

"You're alive," Veronica spoke the words with obvious relief.

"Why wouldn't I be? Just sampled a bit of some very special wine, strong as it is. You go

finish dinner. I'm going to rest here a bit." She turned to her side.

"Oh, and I prepared the dry ingredients, just drop in the rest of whatever."

"Sure, Ma'am Julia." Veronica vowed to become rich one day. Being a good girl was nice, but it didn't pay the bills, she had to step up the game. *Please forgive me, Father in heaven*, she silently said. Veronica smoothed her fingers across her apron pocket feeling for the piece of paper with the combination code to the safe.

STOLEN TIME

JULIA

A dark shadow appeared, and that voice. A voice she had not heard for months. The one she'd hoped to find answers from. What did it want?

"Hello" it hissed in her ear. "Now that you are ripe, I'm keeping my word. I'm coming for you."

Julia clenched her fists, her own voice surprised her, it came out like a lion's roar. "I want answers. I didn't... I didn't ask for any of this."

"You were easy." Zilda ignored Julia's outburst, then an inhumane laugh penetrated her ears as the shadow took some sort of form.

"I do not know what's happened to today's generation. But your ancestors, they fought us hard."

Julia squinted at the dark silhouette. It was out of focus. Zilda continued. "You, on the other hand... you are something. You even want to kill poor Jack. Boohoo. Frankly, you are almost as rotten as me."

"What are you talking about? You did this to me. You tricked me. You're the one who made me agree to this so-called deal." The unpleasant smell of the witch's old apartment with its lit candles came back to Julia. She looked around and found that she was in the middle of that same room, the same candles burning bright on the same small round table, and with the same, greenish couch with maggots crawling out of the torn fabric. She was dressed in a fancy polished outfit, her hair styled, as usual, jewels gleaming.

"Oh silly girl, don't you like being pampered? Wealthy? Loved?"

The silhouette now took the form of the witch Julia recalled. She still had a massive hunch, bony fingers, missing teeth, wrinkled and lifeless skin. Near death. Zilda stepped in closer until they were nose to nose and took air in through her nostrils for a lengthy amount of time, as if she was about to devour a long-awaited meal. "Smells very wealthy indeed."

Julia's feet locked in place. She couldn't move, let alone run. The repugnant smell of rotten potatoes forced her to hold her breath. "Get away from me, or I will—"

"You will do what, silly? Call the cops? Tell your dear husband the truth?" Zilda extended her dirty fingers to touch Julia's locks, the dirt under Zilda's long nails fell off onto her perfectly styled hair. "Not letting you go silly, not until you hear what I have to say."

"What do you have to say, you she-devil?"

"Oh, dearest. You haven't met the devil yet," the woman said, laughing. She pulled away from Julia's face, picking the maggots out of the couch before she lowered herself to sink into its cushions.

"Now, you listen to me. You are to surrender your child to me when she turns seven years old. You are to do it with no remorse. You shall not try to hide the child from me. If you do, I will turn her into an evil puppet, just like you. Make her life miserable, just like yours, and still eat her soul up, just like yours." She pulled a fattened maggot out from under her thigh and crushed it between the few teeth that remained.

Julia's mouth twisted. She forced herself to swallow the burning, vile stuff. She didn't want to show this creature a single weakness. "A child?"

"Precisely. You are such a fun toy, silly. How amazingly evil you've become." Zilda smiled, popping another maggot into her mouth. "Your jealousy, selfishness, and anger has consumed you. You are on the brink of murder. You are almost as sinful as my kind."

Julia turned red. She felt the heat in her cheeks, just as she'd felt it the night she'd "made a deal" with this wretched beast. And just as they had that night, her fists clenched, and she tried to throw punches at Zilda, but her feet were glued in place and her punches only fell through the air.

Zilda seemed to be done with her snack. She rose, and spat in Julia's face. "Don't you want to know who I am? I think you ought to, as you are picking up right after me."

"I will never be like you," Julia managed to say, willing the nausea back into her gut. She wished she could wipe the maggot spit off her face, but her hands were petrified.

"You are like me. For one, you are trying to kill your darling husband. The man who loves you more than life, thanks to me of course." She let out a very wicked and chilling laugh—the type Julia had only heard in operas or playhouses on Broadway.

"I'm not going to kill him." Julia thought about the poison she placed back in her safe, she couldn't go on with it.

"Tsk, not a good move. If you do not kill him, I will."

"You don't scare me. You, sack of rotten worms. Don't you dare touch my Jack. He has nothing, *nothing*, to do with this. Just leave us alone. Leave me alone."

"Hmm. You know something? For humans, your parents were nice. Not like you at all. They tried to save you, but it didn't work. And because they tried to run, I cursed them as well as you. You forgot your parents because that is what I willed. You were a homeless orphan because that is what I willed. Your soul was to be mine when you turned seven. But your parents did not want to give you up, hence your suffering, Julia." The witch looked in the mirror next to the small round table, touching her creased face.

"Now you see, I am old. Withering away. That is because of *your* foolish parents. Your payment for their mistake is your suffering and of course your daughter's life on the day she turns seven."

Julia remembered the locket, and her parent's pictures and the written phrase, "Pure love breaks evil." Maybe this was what her parents wanted to tell her. That the only way to destroy Zilda was through pure love. But how? Certainly, no human could love that woman. No. it had to be another method.

"Who the hell are you?" Julia asked, bewildered.

Zilda plopped back on the couch, this time investigating her nails and picking out the dirt from underneath them.

"I'm the spirit of another world, but your ancestors called us witches. I do prefer the term 'spirit' though. Your ancestors are Ortors. Some of us were able to survive by extracting Ortor souls when they were of age, and we lived on eternally through your generations. We have our world down below, and it can't survive without the human blood that your kind—you Ortors—have tried to stop us from collecting."

"What? I've done no such thing. And what is this chatter about? Are you saying I'm an Ortor?"

"Hardly. A powerless one, just like your mother." The witch brushed her wart-covered fingers against her dead looking face, then she sprang up and walked to the round table.

"What do you know of my mother?" Julia demanded once more.

"Enough of this talk. How about I tell you, yet again, that you will not have to kill your lover boy, because I shall do it myself. I want to see your pain."

"I told you, maggot filth; I'm not killing anybody. I am not succumbing to this game of yours. Frankly," Julia paused for a moment then said, "I'm done being your puppet. I will allow Jack to see his children. I will do anything for him, even go back to being homeless."

"No, Silly Julia. You will never change, you will be consumed by jealousy, anger, and hatred all your life. Because that is what I willed.

There is no turning back from it, no running from it. Your destiny has been set."

"I *will* change and do everything in my power to reverse this," Julia said through clenched teeth. "And I told you I'm not killing anybody. Especially not my husband. Not anymore. So don't count on it."

"That's fine. You might have heard me mention this, but you do not have to kill him because, as I said, I will." The witch let out a long screech.

"Leave him out of this!"

"Oh, silly girl, the evil must continue in this pathetic little world, otherwise it's no fun!"

"Stop it," Julia screamed. "Stop it. Stop it. Stop it!"

"Shh, shh, shh, love," Jack's sweet voice penetrated through her horror.

"Oh Jack." She threw herself at him, circling her arms around his neck.

"Bad dream again?"

"Yes, and too much wine I guess." Julia smiled and attempted to get off the couch. She looked into his deep blue eyes and drew in their comfort and warmth. "I love you. You are my hero, my savior. You are my life."

Jack beamed with pride before helping her off the couch. "Take it easy there Julia." With a happy gallop in his voice, he added, "Veronica cooked up a storm." Julia joined him at their mahogany dining room table, which was illuminated by a dim chandelier, and they took their first bites of a delicious meal.

"Jack." She put her hands on his. "I'm so sorry for the way I've acted all these years. The way I reacted when you mentioned your children, the selfish and angry attitude you must deal with. You didn't deserve any of it."

"Julia. Don't." He put his index finger in front of his mouth. "I understand. I do. You need time. It's a huge deal. And you know what? That's fine with me."

Julia let out a breath. Still feeling guilty, her eyes shifted down to her steak and potatoes. "You've been nothing but amazing to me. I'm ready to meet your children and let them fully into our lives. For myself and for us."

❧

"Dinner was great, Veronica. Thank you," Jack called out, smiling as he watched Julia lick the chocolate souffle off her spoon.

"Ah. Is it ok, if I go, Sir and Ma'am Roe? It is getting a bit late," Veronica asked in a low trembling voice, sweat gleaming down her forehead.

"No, no, you are staying in the butler's quarters today. It's far too late for you to go home at this hour," Jack said in a firm tone.

"Thank you, Sir Jack." She ironed her palms against her white apron.

"Veronica. You can call me Jack. We tell you all the time you can simply call us just Jack and Julia."

"I'm so sorry, I'm used to it from my previous employers, they liked formal naming. I will try to stick to your first names only." Veronica gave a soft, shy smile and began clearing the table.

Julia yawned. "I don't know about you, but I'm exhausted."

"I sure am, too. Let's get some rest. Tomorrow is an exciting day for us, you get to meet my–" Jack looked up at the ceiling, smiling, "I mean *our* children."

"Tell me a bit about them?" she asked. She only knew that he had two boys and a girl.

"Well, the two boys are quite different from one another. For example, you can tell that Caiden will grow up to be someone powerful, specifically in the business world."

"Just like his daddy, huh?" Julia smiled, brushing her fingers over his jawline.

"Perhaps." Jack shrugged. "He constantly asks me to tell him about the real estate business and loves to learn about the jewelry trade when he is in my showrooms." Jack pleasantly smiled. "I see him taking over my businesses one day and running them successfully."

"So, Caiden will pick up after you. What about the other boy?"

"I do think Caiden will. One day I am sure he will open his own jewelry line. He's only six, but so determined. Well, his brother is his polar opposite. More relaxed and so loving. He loves to play house with his sister and to decorate anything he gets his hands on."

The thought of his three-year-old son put a soft smile across his face. "And your daughter?"

"Oh, she's still a baby, she'll always be my baby. Her name is Layla. You'll meet all of them tomorrow." Jack looked at the time. "Let's go to bed."

Julia ran upstairs. "I'm hopping in the shower, but don't you fall asleep until I get back," she tried to convey her implication with a smirk.

Jack was waiting for her when she emerged from the shower room. When she dropped her towel to the floor, she noticed how Jack stirred in bed, eyes alight with need as his gaze settled on her bare breasts and trailed down lower. With a tease, she walked toward the bed. From underneath the silk sheets, her eyes picked up on a very specific hint, his need for her. He climbed out of bed, lifted her off her feet, and carried her back. As he cupped her breasts in his large hands, he slyly bit her lower lip. As he prepared to enter her in the typical position, she pushed him away and flipped her body over to sit atop him, his most gentle and needy appendage between her legs. She took charge, demanding that she have him her way this time. She rocked and circled her hips until he could no longer resist the release.

He fell asleep in short order, his breath steady and peaceful. Every time she watched him sleep, she felt as if she were laying on a grass field full of sunflowers, enjoying a perfect breeze from a nearby beach.

As she ran her fingers back and forth through his messy red curls, she thought about how hard it was for her to accept the fact that his children came first. But she was determined to change, to be close to him, to them. After taking in his pleasantness, she decided it was time to tell Jack the truth, about everything. About the old witch, about the spell. Everything. And if he didn't believe her, at least she'd have the burden off her shoulders and she'd know she'd told him the truth. And if he decided to leave her for it, then it would be for the better.

Not wanting to wake him, she gave his satin lips a kiss and got out of bed. She went back into the washroom and tightened her cashmere robe around her small waist. She splashed cool water onto her face while searching for the words to tell Jack the truth.

VERONICA

Veronica situated herself by the edge of the bed, playing with the piece of paper that had 6982 scribbled on it. Folding and unfolding it about twenty times over and over. Her palms broke into a sweat. Ten minutes passed, then twenty, thirty, one hour. She was sure she'd given them enough time to fall asleep.

Pinching her long, slightly see-through nightgown between her index finger and thumb, she raised it a bit above her ankles. Paper still clenched in her fist, Veronica tiptoed down the stairs from the butler quarters to the first floor of the house, careful not to make a peep. After reaching the living room, she stopped, held her breath, and listened for footsteps from the third-floor master bedroom. Nothing but quiet. She felt at ease as she realized how unlikely it was that her employers would hear her moving about in their massive home. She brushed the sweat off her large forehead and tiptoed anyway. One could never be too careful. They were fast asleep, she reminded herself over and over, continuing her journey through the living room. As she stared down the marble stairway to the cellar, she felt her heart race, along with her mind. What if she was caught? What if there was something horrible in there? What if that bitch Julia came down for another one of her rich people's wines? But she pushed on, shaking like a leaf. She reminded herself that she needed this money for her father.

JULIA

Julia straightened her posture as she patted her cheeks dry with a soft towel. She was ready to reveal the truth. Over and over, she practiced her words as she walked toward their bed.

"Jack," she called faintly, a few feet away from their bed.

No answer.

"Jack, I must tell you something," she called out again, this time a little louder. In the back of her mind, she thought that she may be with him for the last time right then, and how this might be her last day in her beautiful home. The last time anyone called her "Mrs. Roe." She no longer cared. She had to stop caring if she wanted to keep Jack safe from the witch. If she wanted to be cleansed of her lies.

"Jack you might reject what I must say now." She was ready to jump into bed and shake him awake. "Jack love, I know I wore you out earlier tonight." She giggled. "Really, I must talk to you now, or I will never have the strength to do it again." Usually, he was a light sleeper, but not tonight.

"Come on," she persisted, leaning in closer, caressing his bare shoulder, which peeked out from the silk sheets. He felt stiff, motionless, and cold.

She knew but she didn't want to believe it.

A hint of panic escaped her lips "JACK!" she screamed, shaking him.

No response.

"NO. NO. NO!" Julia screamed. Tears poured down her cheeks, and her body felt numb. For a few seconds, she lost her senses, her vision blurred, and the room spun around her. She could not hear or see. Her body shook in a cold sweat, then she felt a burning heat rise to her head. She could not think. All she could do was Scream. Scream. Scream.

❦

Veronica heard a loud shriek from upstairs and stopped in her tracks. "What happened now?" She was so close... another step, and she would be down those stairs. Not wanting to take any chances, she tiptoed back to the living room, and stood by the couch to listen. She was almost sure that a few seconds ago she'd heard Ma'am Julia. She decided to stay in the living room for a bit, and worried that she had not imagined those screams.

❦

Julia wanted to shake Jack again and again, but she couldn't touch him. Not now. Not like this. Her voice was trapped in her fear, her tongue stuck to the roof of her mouth. She could not utter a word. She watched his chest, hoping to see it rise and fall. He was still and pale. His lips had turned from lively red to a pale blue.

She tried to calm herself. Shaky, anxious to feel his body, she finally placed her index and middle finger on his neck to feel for a pulse. Nothing. She tried his wrist. Nothing. As she gently released his hand, she noticed how heavy it was; it dropped down to the side of the bed like a log.

Tears ran down her cheeks, loud sobs penetrated the room until her mouth and throat were dry and even then, she could not move. She could only wail in weak whines.

Julia's, her heart sank. She was unable to maintain any measure of calm numbness, unable to fight the pain. She felt like nothing mattered. Emptiness and loneliness overwhelmed her mind.

"Help, someone Help!"

No, Veronica had not imagined it. Something had happened. As she was about to go back upstairs, every muscle in her body clenched with panic, she remembered the paper crushed in her hand. Veronica looked around the massive living room, and the first possible hiding place she laid eyes on was a white couch with decorative crystals. In haste, she stuffed the paper deep inside one of the creases and covered it with a pillow. She lifted her nightgown to her knees and dashed up the stairs to her employer's bedroom.

Veronica didn't bother knocking. She swung the doors open, and gasped at the sight of her fathead boss, looking so broken and in a way so normal. Normal, like other human beings, capable of crying, feeling. Julia was drowning in tears, on the floor, next to the bed. Her face cupped in her own hands, sobbing.

"Is he...?" Veronica asked, holding onto her nightgown, tiptoeing into the bedroom.

Julia's sobs pierced the room.

"What? How?" Veronica covered her mouth, to prevent gagging.

Julia just shook her head.

"We must call the police," Veronica said firmly, taking a confident stance, the stance of authority.

Julia nodded. Veronica's heart sank, as she took another look at Sir Jack. Her eyes filled with tears.

"Sir Jack was a wonderful man," she sobbed. "He respected everyone, even me. He was kind, he was a special person, and you, Ma'am Julia..." Veronica's voice took a furious tone. "I can't believe you would do such a horrible thing to your husband, a man who loved you more than anything in this world." She spoke as if she finally freed herself from invisible shackles.

Julia stopped sobbing for a minute, removed her hands from her face, and turned to Veronica in bewilderment. Veronica stared back, she was sure her eyes were fiery with rage and maybe with fear.

"I'll tell the police everything," she announced, not taking her eyes off Julia.

"Tell them everything about what?" Julia asked.

"Don't you look at me with that fake innocence." Veronica pointed a finger at her, keeping her distance at the bedroom door. "I know you did it. I didn't want to believe it, but I know you did. You killed your husband. You're a murderer."

Julia shook her head. "Veronica, you have to listen to me." Julia pushed off the floor with her arms for support. "You have to believe me. I did not kill my husband." Bitch looked like she'd been electrocuted, and the shock traveled to every bone. She didn't have the strength to rise from the bedroom floor. Her knees obviously trembled. Veronica saw how Julia struggled. How she stared at her dead husband, still kneeling at his side. Veronica saw how Julia used any strength she had to try and convince her that she was wrong, that Julia had done nothing.

"Why would I commit such a horrid crime? I loved him. Don't ever say things like this. You hear me?"

"Loved him." Veronica scoffed. "You just wanted his money, or whatever else your agenda was. I know women like you very well. You fake affection for your men to get what you want. You are liars and thieves, every last one of you."

"Veronica, you are shocked right now. So am I. I just lost the love of my life." Julia attempted to get up once more and managed. She approached. For the briefest moment, Veronica felt bad for Ma'am. But she didn't want to lose control. She couldn't give control back to Julia.

"Listen to me, Veronica—"

"Don't get any closer, murderer!" Veronica yelled, standing her ground. She felt her eyebrows draw close together. Stretching her hand out in front of Julia's face, she gestured for Julia to stop talking.

Julia took another slow step toward her. "Veronica," she tried, calm and steadily, "I need to call the police and ambulance right now. I must call for help. Please, please try to help me here." She gestured toward the phone. It was atop the dresser, near where Veronica stood.

Veronica made a quick movement to the phone. "That's right, call the police, or better yet..." she snatched the phone from the bedroom dresser. "I will do it myself."

Veronica waved the phone in front of Julia's face. "I know all about your little safe in the cellar, what sort of weapons do you keep down there? When the police get here, I will show them everything. They will arrest you. You horrible, horrible woman."

Julia took a baby step forward. Veronica noticed the clarity and sharpness in Julia's eyes. Anger.

"My safe? So, you've been snooping around?"

"Don't come any closer." *Oh God, one oh mighty Father in heaven, help me get through this.* "It doesn't matter now." Veronica scoffed. "You are an evil person. Killing your husband like that for money."

"You know nothing. For the last time, I didn't kill him. The witch, she killed him. She told me in the dream earlier that she would make us miserable. She told me she would kill him. Yes. She did it." Julia laughed hysterically, with tears in her eyes.

"*You're* the witch. Talking crazy, too. You lost your mind, and I'm telling the police that, too." Not taking her eyes off Julia, Veronica, raised the phone, and frantically began dialing.

"Oh no, you're not." Julia sprang toward Veronica, grabbing her hand, and knocking the phone away.

"Let go of me, you witch. I will expose you," Veronica screamed, shaking off Julia's hand. She tried to fight her mistress, and she managed to scratch Julia's face, leaving a bloody mark just below her left eye. She took a firm stance next to the bedroom dresser. She was determined, and her cheeks swelled even more with rage.

It came as a surprise when Veronica felt Julia's thin hand slap her across the face with all her might, and she felt a hard push in the middle of her chest. Veronica lost her balance before she could strike back. She tripped over her nightgown. She felt the crown of her head hit the corner of the bedroom dresser. She fell to the floor, slightly twitching, and then she could not move at all.

BREAKTHROUGH II

ANGELA
Fall
Early 1970s

The letter slipped through Angela's small fingers, she began to tremble and felt sick to her stomach. She picked it up and looked it over again. She hid the first page in her pocket and ran upstairs, hand over her mouth, trying not to puke. So many thoughts rushed through her mind.

I'm an Ortor? Zilda raised me and lied about my parents. The famous Jack Roe... my father... that makes Liam my half-brother. Which makes Caiden my half-brother. Oh, God!

"What is it? Tell me?" Liam jumped off the couch as soon as he saw Angela.

Angela ran to the bathroom and threw up. After splashing her face with cold water, she was able to focus a little better. She looked at her reflection, but it didn't seem right. Nothing did. Everything was wrong, off, misplaced. The world had shifted off-axis.

Once she finally found the strength to speak, she found Liam standing by the door, mouth open.

"I'm sorry, Liam."

"For what?"

She didn't move. Liam helped her to the living room and sat her down on the couch. He returned with a tall glass of water.

An hour passed before Liam finally broke the silence. "You're obviously not ok. I want to help you, and if you don't tell me what's going on, I will go down there and find out myself."

Angela held her hand out, motioning for him not to go. She handed him the second page of the letter, trying to read the expression on his face as he skimmed through its words.

When he was done, his face was expressionless. No one moved or said a word. Liam turned to Angela with tears in his eyes. "Hi, sis."

Angela was surprised by how calm and composed Liam was. He just learned that it was her mother who destroyed his happy family. And was responsible for the murder, and the horrid dumping of his father's body. As they tried to make sense of things, hours passed, without notice it was 6:00 p.m., and the sound of the phone stirred them back to the present. Angela got up to answer.

Before she could say anything, the caller spoke first. "Hello, Angela" a deep voice said on the other line.

"Caiden." Angela sighed, feeling ill again. Caiden seemed to ignore or not notice the lack of enthusiasm in her voice.

"I'm picking you up in about an hour?" She could hear the excitement, the anticipation in his voice.

She had forgotten about their date. "No, I'm sorry Caiden. I can't make it. I can't." She hung up the phone.

Liam was casually standing by the kitchen door, one leg crossed over the other. He looked her up and down, calm as a leaf that just slowly and gracefully fell off a dry tree branch.

"My brother, I suppose?"

"*Our* brother," Angela corrected, holding a hand to her mouth.

"Did you cancel a date with him?"

"Are you serious? Of course I did. I'm about to puke all over your bell-bottoms."

The phone rang again. Angela whipped it from the receiver. "Hello," she snapped.

"I think we got disconnected." His voice was like honey to her soul. *NO*, she thought. Without saying a word, she hung up again.

"So... I take it you're not going to go out with him?" Liam asked.

This shocked her. "Are you out of your mind?"

"I saw the way you two looked at each other that night, no doubt there is something, or should I say everything there."

"After what we just found out. How can you even? Angela made a spitting sound, she approached Liam, and with a punch, pushed him out of the way, and walked upstairs. She wanted to disappear.

Liam followed her. "You don't understand Angela," he said, but she didn't want to hear it. She was too frustrated to listen to another word. She had to think about other things, like finding the body, finishing her story, or just disappearing for a while.

"Just listen to me," Liam insisted and tried again. "What we just found out is crazy. The fact that we are related. And you can finish working your story." He continued to follow her as she tried to hide in one of the rooms. She hoped to lock him out.

"The thing is Angela. I think you and Caiden have something special, and you should not worry about him being—"

Angela cut him off. "I never thought I would say this to you Liam, but that's just sick." She was sure this was the first time she'd ever snapped at him.

She couldn't stop yelling. All the emotion, all the information, everything she found out about her mother, about Zilda, her father, her magic. Her heart pounded. She felt tingling in her stomach, and she knew she could make everything go away with a wave of her hand. Her powers were strong, and she remembered how to use them. She flushed red, she was ready to strike, to make him forget, make herself forget all the bad, all the wrong. Instead, she flung Liam across the hallway. He was about three feet in the air; he flew from room to room until his body gently landed at the end of the hall. Remorse came over her for a moment. She had only meant for Liam to leave her alone. She hadn't meant to send him flying down the hallway. She had to learn to control her powers, but she didn't know how. She started toward Liam but didn't quite make it all the way there. The ground shook, and her mind took her to that dark place again. That metallic forest. A place close to the core of the earth. She recalled the warnings from her real mother's letter. She wasn't to use magic. Well, it was too late to put that toothpaste back in the tube, and now she stared at this awful chasm right in her home that existed because she'd used magic. She saw the earth above open, and something ugly crawled from the crevice before quickly retreating back inside.

The chasm closed, and she heard Liam speak. "What happened?"

"You sorta fainted," she lied.

"Really? I've never fainted in my life. Don't remember being faint of heart." She was glad he still maintained his sense of humor. He wasn't angry. But she still was.

"You probably fainted because this is our brother you're talking about. I don't even want to think about this. Don't mention it again!" She left him on the floor, and stomped downstairs, letting out a long breath. She needed to get away from him. She had to stop thinking about using magic, figure out a way to control it. Stop. Stop thinking. Thinking about Jack Roe, Caiden, Zilda Julia. Stop it all. She knew she shouldn't use the powers. The one time in her life when she wanted to do it, really wanted to... she couldn't. She heard Liam approach her again.

"Do you understand Liam? Never, ever mention Caiden again."

Liam ignored her. The nerve of the man made her blood boil.

"Have you noticed that he looks different from me, Layla, my mother, and from you? His olive skin, his dark hair and eyes?

Angela walked in circles around the mansion. Up and down the staircase, in and out of the bedrooms, and back and forth down the hallway. She stopped by one of the upstairs bedrooms, dropped her hands to her sides, and sat on the floor in the hallway. After a few moments, she walked over to the spiral staircase down to the living room and stopped by the broken wall. She took a deep breath before approaching the cellar again. She picked up the contents from the safe she'd left on the ground, shoved them away, and slammed the door shut.

As Angela locked the safe, she mumbled to Liam. "All this is too much for me. Do you understand? You *think* Jack Roe is not his father? That Caiden and I *might* not be siblings? Is that good enough?" She turned to him to face him. For the first time, she noticed a hint of sadness and maybe even panic in his eyes. "So, this is what I've decided to do. After the body is confirmed, I will conclude the story of Jack Roe in my next column. I will write a letter to your mother explaining everything the best I can."

Angela turned off the flashlight. Once upstairs, she continued to lay out her plan. Liam followed her and listened to her quietly.

"After I do my last report on the case, I'm leaving the country. Just to take a break from all this."

"And where are you going to go?"

"I don't know. England? France? Italy maybe?"

"You have just discovered you have a family. Don't you want to be part of this family? Is that what you really want to do? Run when you can't cope with your own emotions?"

"Family? Do you think your mother will accept me, after what my mother did to your family? Do you think I can face them?"

A knock interrupted them. Angela rushed to open the door. But stopped before answering. She needed a distraction from all this, though she feared Caiden had found his way over. To her relief, Ed stood on the steps.

"I saw your car, decided to stop by," Ed casually welcomed himself in. He looked between Julia and Liam. "An' just why are ya'll in such a down mood?"

"Ed," Angela decided to take a chance and ask, "did you know my real mother? Julia?"

Ed went red in the face. His eyes squinted into small lines.

"You did, didn't you?" Angela said, clenching her teeth "Why did you lie to me? All these years! lies, lies, lies!"

Ed wiped the sweat off his face and sighed.

"I did. I lied to ya, an' I sure am sorry."

CLEANING UP THE MESS

JULIA
Summer
1940s

The moon hid itself, and the grey vapor of the clouds extinguished the starlit sky. Julia sat motionless next to the mahogany bed, barely blinking, face wet from crying. Her right hand rested on Jack's cold forehead. Her mind was somewhere far away, in an empty hall, devoid of color. A few feet from her, Veronica lay in a pool of blood. Her white nightgown was stained a rosy pink.

"Bravo, Julia! To kill is to become heartless. You are learning very well, child, better than expected." Zilda's voice shook Julia back to reality. "What? You have nothing to say now? Money and fake love were so important to you. You neglected your true self."

"What have I done? What have I done?" Julia cried to no one.

The witch laughed.

"Shut up and leave me alone. No. You know what, go ahead and kill me. You won, whatever you wanted to achieve have did, and whoever you wanted to hurt, you have. I don't care about anything anymore. You won."

"Oh, but we are not quite done yet."

"Yes, we are. I'm calling the police." Julia's mind exited the empty colorless hall, and she found herself in her bedroom, able to think once again.

"Ah, interesting. And what are you going to tell them? That you found your husband and housemaid dead in your bedroom? With blood on your hands?" the witch hissed, with a hint of pleasure.

"I said I don't care about any of it. They can jail me for life!" Julia screamed. She wondered if she was imagining things or talking to herself because she did not *see* Zilda. She was finally able to get to her feet. When her eyes once again crossed Veronica's body, she trembled. She could have never imagined she would find herself surrounded by dead bodies. She had to ignore the voice. She was imagining it. Had to be.

The witch read her mind. "No, you're not imagining things, I promise."

Drumming her forehead with her finger, Julia said to herself, "Get out of my head! I'm not crazy, I'm not crazy." She took the necessary steps to Veronica's body and picked up the phone to dial the police.

"You don't want to do that," the voice said.

Julia ignored it.

"You don't want to do that." The voice became clearer as the room turned dark. A murky shadow appeared, and there she was. Zilda stood before Julia, clear as day. Just as she'd remembered her.

Julia took a few steps back.

"You don't want to call the authorities, because once they arrest you, who will take care of the baby?" The witch tilted her head to look at Julia's belly.

"Baby?"

"Yes. The one that belongs to me."

Julia laughed. "You're insane. I am not with child. You're lying," she said.

The witch reached out and placed her hand on Julia's belly. Julia expected pain to accompany the horrid woman's touch, but instead, she felt warmth in her abdomen. The presence of another life. Zilda smiled and removed her hand from Julia's body. "You see?"

The phone slipped through Julia's hands. It hit the floor with a thud. She put her hands on her flat belly. "This is a trick," she said, but she wasn't so certain she believed that. Everything the witch had predicted the night Julia had followed her into that terrifying building—all of it had come true. This did not bode well for the child, if it would be a girl. Julia understood that, but in her moment of grief, the fleeting warmth of love captured her heart.

"Baby?" she repeated with a slight smile, but then tears filled her eyes, overflowing then rapidly streaming down her small face.

"You killed my husband, you maggot tramp! There is no chance for happiness anymore. His children will never know what happened to him. My child will never know a father!"

"Oh, save the dramatics. Clean this mess and live your life, silly. You have seven years to enjoy with her until I come back to claim her."

"Her? I'm going to have a girl?" She rubbed her belly. Then darkness overwhelmed her again, as she took a glimpse at her lifeless husband's body.

Zilda followed Julia's eyes. "I do think you should clean this party up," she said with a laugh.

Julia's hands shook. "You made this mess. You clean it up, old bag"

"Sorry, I don't clean messes. I only create them. But I will see you in seven," the witch said as she snapped her bony fingers. The air cleared, the darkness dissipated, and Julia alone with Jack and Veronica.

She sat back down on the floor and tried to produce a plan. Calling the cops made no sense; at least two hours had passed since the deaths. No one would believe Julia about the witch anyway—and to top it off, she was carrying a child. Being locked up in jail with a belly was not an option. Doing what was best for her and the child did not involve phoning the police.

The clouds seemed to drift from the full moon, exposing its yellowish glow, which lit Jack's face with a tender hue of orange. He almost looked alive.

"I'm sorry, my love," she cried. "I'm so sorry." After a few minutes, she stood to face the cold scene. She couldn't stomach looking at Jack anymore. Not another second. She covered his body with a sheet and turned to Veronica.

She wiped tears from her face as she took another bedsheet and placed it on the floor. She had retrieved gloves from the servant's quarter and slipped them on. She walked over to Veronica. Julia cursed as she prepared herself. She decided to treat Veronica gently. And as she rolled the body on to the sheet, she wished the idea of treating her servant well had occurred to her earlier. Now, Veronica would endure the same tormented treatment Julia always gave her. She would never know that Julia could be kind and loving. She had not been. The witch was not wrong. Julia had been selfish. Heartless. She no longer knew who she was or what she was.

She wrapped Veronica up in the sheet and tied it with a rope. She fell to the floor. Devoid of any strength, she tried to catch her breath. She knew she needed to do the same with Jack's body, but the thought sent shivers down her spine and an upheaval through her gut. Her food from the night before was at her feet before she knew it was happening. She barely glanced at it and began to wonder how she could possibly get them down those staircases.

Julia looked around the room. She could not handle the bodies on her own. They were too heavy, and she was too small. One person popped into her mind who she thought could be persuaded and trusted to help her. Before she ran out the door to find him, she looked over toward

Jack's covered body. Her heart rose to her throat. She had no more tears left. "I'm sorry I have to do this to you, Jack. I will never forgive myself."

The stars shimmered naively in the dark sky. The frigid wind hit Julia's face on her run to her car before she jumped inside and started its engine. She drove slowly down the many silent streets of Long Island. Then she arrived in Manhattan, a place that felt familiar. She drove down 51st, 52nd, and around again.

"Where are you?" she repeated for an hour as she drove in circles. As she was about to give up, she spotted a thin body with an oversized hat and an undersized jacket. He was on 50th, trying to start a fire with two large twigs. Julia abruptly stopped her car, swung her door open, and ran out to him.

"Jules? Tha' ya?" The man squinted. Tumbling from side to side, he tried to walk toward her but toppled over onto the ground.

A grin spread across his face. "Lookin' good, lil' lady. Wha' ya doin' here? Haven' seen ya in foreva'."

He looked much older, worn-out almost. A few years earlier, she was able to see his dimples, but now they were hidden in a cluster of wrinkles. His smile had not changed, though. Julia was always surprised by the amount of joy he showed. After all, he was a homeless bum. What was there to be happy about?

"Ed, my old friend." She looked down at her polished shoes, making a small well with them in the soft earth. "I need your help."

Ed lowered himself onto his square piece cardboard. Julia lifted her wool skirt and sank next to him. Taking a deep breath, she looked him straight in the eyes.

"I may be a bit dizzy fizzy," he hiccupped, "but I do see ya mean business lil' lady."

Julia shielded her nose from his sour-smelling alcohol breath. "This won't be easy."

Ed rested his head on a large green dumpster. "An' how can I help ya? I got nothing. 'Cept this, o' course." He reached behind the dumpster and pulled out a big half-empty bottle of Jack Daniels. "Just like ol' times. Let's have a drink. I'm bein' generous today." He took a big gulp and extended his hand to Julia. "Rememba' our song? C'mon sing with me."

Julia rolled her eyes. Brushing dirt off her shoes.

Ed didn't seem to notice her irritation and fell into a tune within seconds.

> *"It's summa time, Oh. Yeah. I don' need no gloves.*
> *So wha' if I got holes in my dirty socks.*
> *No one cares about me anyway.*
> *It's summa time, Oh. Yeah. I don' need no shoes.*
> *So wha' if my jeans are loose?*
> *I got my bottle and my cig, and a little bite to eat*
> *That's all I need, that's all I need.*
> *It's summa time in New York City, people go about their day*
> *An' no one cares about me anyway.*
> *I got my bottle and my cig, and a little bite to eat*
> *That's all I need, that's all I need."*

He sighed and smiled. Took another drink.

"It was hard, gettin' this bottle, ya know. It's the most expensive I ever got. Collected the ol' coin for few weeks now. Let's celebrate." He smiled and lit up a cigarette.

"I'm not here for the drink Ed," she replied, then thought better of it. "Well, ok. Maybe I am." She grabbed the bottle and took a giant gulp. She looked up into the dark sky. "I need you to help me do something, and I promise I will buy you twenty bottles if you wish."

He lifted the red floppy hat so that the brim was above his eyes. "Is tha' so?" he asked. "I'm all ears." He took a puff of his Marlboro.

"Yes, Ed. I'll even buy you shoes and socks, so you can stay warm for the winter and a jacket. A jacket that will actually fit you properly."

Ed looked at his torn shoes, and rubbed his scruffy white beard, but he didn't need much convincing "Alrigh' then, what ya need, Jules?"

"Get in the car. I'll explain everything soon." She lifted herself and adjusted her skirt to carefully step over the twig fire. She was impressed by how comfortable she still was with the streets. For a moment, it was as though she never left them. She'd finally woken from her dream to a nightmare.

"An automobile! Excitin'." Ed lazily got up, cradling the bottle in his hands.

"Hurry. We don't have much time."

⚜

When they reached the mansion, Ed's eyes lit up. "Golly. Where this comin' from?" The shock of what he saw seemed to sober him up a bit.

"Don't ask too many questions," Julia warned.

"With pleasure, lil' lady." He curtsied, taking his cap off. "I'll show respect fo' the lady. It's summa time... ooo... ooo... ooo... I don' need no gloves... who cares if I got holes in my soooooooocks..."

Julia rolled her eyes. "Be quiet."

"Come on, lil' lady, I know we didn't see each other often, but remember' we used to partna' up to steal booze to keep warm in the winta'? And huddle 'round the fire, makin' up songs to be laughin'? Why you bein' so sour now?"

"I'm being sour, because of what you're about to see." Julia stopped for a moment trying to figure out how to tell Ed that he would see two bodies, one of which was bloodied. She took a long breath and let the air out slowly before she locked eyes with him. "When you see what you're about to see, don't ask questions, or else my offer is off the table."

"Wha' offer?" he asked. Julia knew he had not forgotten her original offer, but that he had decided to up the ante. And that was fine with her.

"Help me with this, and I will change your life for the better forever. You will never live on the streets again."

As much as she didn't want to go back up to her bedroom, she had to hurry before the night slipped away. Julia dashed up the stairs and into her bedroom. Ed followed behind, eyes wide, mouth closed, except when he wanted to take a sip from his bottle.

Julia stopped by her bedroom door. "Don't get scared and yell, Ed. This is bad. This is horrid."

She stepped inside the bedroom, Ed followed close behind, smile wide, bottle by his lips.

"Here we go."

The bottle almost slipped, as Ed gasped and stuttered. "I've seen a lo' on them streets, Jules. But this?" he turned away from the bodies.

"Please."

"Change my life foreva was right, lil' lady. I want no part of this." Ed sprinted for the door.

Julia ran ahead of him and closed the door, pinning her body flush against it. "Ed! Please! Just trust me, for old times' sake. Help me. Help me get these bodies downstairs and into the car."

"Nah, lil' lady, I don' thin' I'll do by you this time."

"If you don't help me..." Julia stopped for a moment and rubbed her belly. "I need you. I have no one else. Just trust me, no one will ever know about this. I need you, my unborn baby needs you. I have no one else to help me." She was begging now, ready to fall to her knees and beg forever.

Ed stopped to look at her. Confused. "A baby?"

"Yes."

Ed sighed. "I ain't one to ask many a question, but how the hella ya get into them mess?"

"It doesn't matter now. Will you help me or not? I promise, I will pay you for this. Five thousand in cash, and I will set you up for life. A new life." She got down on her knees, holding her palms together. "Please," she begged. She felt all strength leave her body. She couldn't think, she couldn't breathe. She kept telling herself to keep it together, if not for herself then for her baby.

Ed took a giant gulp from his bottle. "If it was just you, nah. Don't think I would. But you got the baby on the way, an' who know what else? So yeah, I'll help ya, but only once. Ya can't go around killin' people all over an' expect me to cover ya ass, ok?"

Julia sighed. "Thank you. Thank you so much. No, this will never happen again. I'm not—" *I'm not a murderer*, she thought. That's what she was going to say, but it just wasn't true. "I'll never hurt a fly. I'll never harm anyone. I promise. This isn't *me*. It's because of me, ok? But this isn't me. So, you'll do it?"

Ed took another gulp from his jug. "Let's get on wit' it, then."

❧

The night was sad and cold. After loading the car with the bodies and some heavy-duty rope, they took a wordless drive to Treasure Cove Lake. Once on the bridge, near the trees, the car came to a slow stop.

"We need large rocks," Julia commanded. Ed nodded and quickly gathered the biggest boulders he could roll onto the bridge.

"Now unwrap the sheet from the bottom and tie a rock to each ankle with this." She fumbled in the trunk and waved the rope in front of Ed's face. The redness of a drunkard faded, and his cheeks went pale.

"Oh, I don' thin'..." Ed hesitated.

"You've come this far, and I—I just can't do it. He was my husband." She pointed her finger to one of the sheets.

"How in the world. And who was tha'? Smaller. She a woman, tha's fo' sure. They havin' a affair?" He eyed the other bloody sack.

"No, they weren't. Please, Ed. Remember, no questions? Just do as I say, I promise no one will ever know you were a part of this." Julia didn't mind that she had to continue to beg him. Her situation warranted begging.

The sky turned a lighter shade of blue. The bodies sank as soon as they hit the water. While Julia watched the lake settle from the ripples of lifeless invaders, her heart dropped, and her head spun; she had to steady herself on the bridge rail. Turning to Ed, she placed a finger on her lips.

"Not a word to anybody," she managed to say, "or else you end up in jail, and lose my offer."

She snatched the half-empty bottle from his trembling hands and threw it in the river. "No more of this garbage."

"We work on the specifics later, but ya can' just go tossin' a man's drink in the river like tha'."

"Ed, you don't need it. Taper off. You'll be better for it. Please, I know this was a horrible thing, but it's a second chance for you. Take it. The whole chance, not just pieces of it. I want you to be well."

"Makin' me drown—"

Julia shushed him. "Remember? Never again. This never happened."

For the first time, Ed was at a loss for words. He took off his hat and wiped the sweat from his bald head. He followed Julia to the car.

TO ASHES

JULIA
Spring
1940s

Almost a full year had passed, and the thought of Jack's stiff, lifeless body haunted her day and night. She missed him. She took a deep breath and turned to the wooden crib. The soft pink strokes of color Julia painted on the beige wood had been a personal touch for her daughter's sleeping space.

Baby Angela breathed peacefully. Her deep pink bowtie lips moved in a sucking motion around a fallen pacifier.

"Sleep my girl, sleep," Julia whispered. She left the room as quiet as a butterfly, to say her goodbyes to the mansion, the place she had called home for a few sweet years.

The cellar was the last place in the house she visited. She climbed down the extended stairs to her secret place and approached the wall that showcased her favorite paintings, but this time she did not stop to appreciate the art. Instead, she pulled out an envelope from her skirt pocket and locked it securely away in the safe behind *The Woman in Blue Reading a Letter*.

"This is for you, my little Angel," she whispered to herself.

She went back up the marble staircase to the nursery and peeked into Angela's room, ensuring she was still asleep. Julia began to pack her belongings. As she folded Angela's little clothes into the suitcase, she felt relieved. Leaving this place infused her heart with hope; new beginnings were always heartwarming.

Thankfully, they had enough to sustain themselves for their entire lives. Jack made sure that his possessions, including fifty percent of his real estate and jewelry business, were transferred to Julia. Of course, she had taken precautions after his death and changed her last name. She'd chose to be Julia Wise, a widow of a supposedly prosperous Italian businessman. Julia found that money was more powerful than any law, therefore, she was able to find someone to change her name and forge all her other documents.

But her name did not matter much now; no one in Spain would know her. She walked over to the dresser and took out two passports, tucking them safely in her handbag she whispered; "All ready, Angel." She picked up Angela. "We are going away my love."

For a moment Angela opened her big green-blue eyes. Once she was snuggled in her mother's arms, she fell back into a deep and comfortable sleep. As if touching a delicate flower, Julia brushed Angela's soft cheek with her fingertips, and held her baby tightly. "You look so much like your father, my Angel." She kissed Angela's forehead before turning toward the door.

"Going somewhere, silly?" a voice of evil enveloped the room.

Julia stopped breathing.

"Oh, dear. Did you underestimate me? Thought you could trick me, and run away like your foolish mother?"

Julia hugged Angela closer to her chest.

"Your mother tried to run too, you know. Oh dear, what were you thinking? Bad choice, very bad choice."

"Angela is not seven yet. And yes, I was leaving. We are going on vacation," Julia snapped. She started, ready to run out the door, but the voice followed, and stopped Julia after just a few steps.

Julia felt something slip away. When she looked down, she found her arms empty. A panicked scream escaped her lungs.

"She's alright. She is back in her crib."

Julia ran up the stairs to Angela's room. She placed her hand on the baby's red curls and moved them away from her soft face.

"So much like your lover-boy, Jack. Big green-blue eyes, curly red hair, dimples to *die* for. Hmm. Yes, so very beautiful indeed."

Julia shot daggers at the witch. "Shut your trap."

Zilda cackled. "So, you are running from me, heh?"

"Yes," Julia said firmly. "But I'm not afraid of you." She stood in front of the crib, emboldened by the strength of her love for her child.

"Oh. You have no powers to defeat me. Just like your mother. Do not let my current form fool you. I am more powerful than you can imagine; I have the powers of other worlds to manipulate my victims in any way I wish to. Unfortunately, I cannot accomplish much in this world. You see, to humans, my form is such an ugly thing to behold—a frightful thing. To mingle with humans I must look the part. And I would rather that part be exceptional." The voice turned into a visible shadow. "I need my youth back."

Julia laughed. "I can't imagine how lovely you must have been as a young woman. Good luck with your endeavors, and I will have you know that I do not need powers to get rid of you. I will do it with my bare hands if I have to."

"Well now. Before you begin... trying to get rid of me with your bare hands..." Zilda burst into wicked laughter. "Let me tell you a little story." The shadow turned into a hunched, old, ugly woman—frail and disintegrating. Her skin dripped off her bones as though it had melted, her eyes were a vomitous yellow, and her bald head oozed pus from the large pores deep in its scalp. She stood right next to Julia; a heavy stench filled her nostrils.

Julia took a step back. The witch took one forward.

"My story is about a mommy. A mommy who had a daughter named Julia. Julia belonged to me. Poor mamma thought she could protect her silly child. Oh, how wrong she was! If only she would have listened to me, she might still have her life. If she had lived, I would have absorbed her human form. Her youth would have belonged to me." The witch took another step closer to Julia.

"So," she continued, "I decided to put a little spell that mother's silly daughter, and I killed her poor parents. Oh, might I mention, they were such good parents to their child. But that is irrelevant; the important part is that their silly daughter grew up in the slums. I watched over her to make sure she stayed put. I even guided poor Jack to be ever-so generous with her. When Julia was ready for my deal, I offered it to her. And she agreed to that deal, thus agreeing to give me her child... well, *sort of*." Zilda shrugged. "But Julia, as silly as she was, tried to run. And she lied." Her eyes sparked with anger. "And you know what happens to those who *lie* to the spirit witch?"

Julia took another step back. She looked back at Angela, who was still sleeping. "What?" she managed to ask.

"Oh, you most certainly know this answer to this," Zilda said, looking Julia in the eyes. Unblinking, Zilda continued, "they die." She tried to straighten up, but her hunch was in the way, she took one small step back. "You know, I am rather tired of this body, and I am tired of playing your games." She raised her shriveled old hands into the air and pointed her index finger straight at Julia.

"Your mother broke her deal with me, and I shall take your life because you have tried the same. You thought you could hide from me in another country?" A cloud of black smoke rose trhough the air.

Julia, helpless and resigned, took one last look at her beautiful daughter. "Who will protect her? She is only a few months old."

"Oh. Why do you care? You're already dead."

Julia's felt bones weakened. Whatever the witch was doing to her, it felt as if her soul was detaching from her body. She mustered as much power as she could to let her voice out, to let it be heard.

"Please, don't hurt my daughter. Please." Her heart felt as though thorny vines had crept up and around it.

"Oh, no worries, girl. I have no need for your human trash yet. I have you for my youth. They say two generations of deal breakers wins me a prize. And you are that prize, silly. I get two for the price of one. Your daughter's time will come. When I need my youth revived, she will revive it."

Tears of blood ran down Julia's face, but all she wanted was at least one more second with Angela. She saw only darkness. A light-headed feeling, as if she'd had too much wine, enveloped her consciousness. The room spun rapidly in a circular pattern. She was still able to hear Zilda's voice, and there was an obvious difference in that tone. The witch's voice was smooth, unbreaking. The sound was melodious, softer. And it grew softer and sweeter Zilda continued her metamorphosis.

Julia attempted to open her eyes to see Angela once more. But she only saw the witch, who would have been unrecognizable if Julia had not just been the subject of her continuous torture. Zilda's face was as youthful as mornings' dew, her skin was a whisper of an undisturbed ocean wave. Youth and life brightened her eyes. A set of bright white, straight teeth were set behind a perfect mouth. Zilda appeared human, just as she had intended. And while Julia hated abhorred that human appearance, she could not help but recognize Zilda's beauty.

"P-p-l-eeeeese," Julia managed to rip the word from her own mouth. Her heart told her to speak, but her body was not compliant. She felt something within herself drift away. Her body sensed a form of heaviness, and the departing lightness felt free. It left her fingers and toes as her extremities shriveled up like prunes.

"Don't worry silly, we are almost done here. Oh, I feel better already." Zilda took loud breaths in.

"J-just k-kee-keep her n-n-name as Angela." Julia took deep, staggering breath, and tried to continue; "give her, give her myyyy riiing," she attempted to show Zilda her engagement ring and wedding band, to hold on a minute longer, to see Angela one last time.

Zilda ceased her excited inhaling and exhaling. "No. Her name shall be Ash. Because that is what you will become, and so will she. I shall remove her soul, and I will take her life. Just as I am taking yours."

"You. old. Tramp." Julia wanted to fight the witch with her words or body. Anything, but not this petrification. She did not know what was worse, her helplessness or the pain.

"Darling, I am no longer old. I would like for you to die knowing that your soul was taken by Zilda."

Julia couldn't answer, couldn't fight anymore. It was too painful to know that she had lost.

She heard a cry somewhere far away. Angela, her beautiful daughter, was crying for her mother, a mother who would never nurse her child again.

The cries drifted farther away until all Julia heard was a gush of what sounded like wind. It was soft, bitter, and light. She drifted away with it as it sent her somewhere—to a place that was bright and dark at the same time.

Julia's life flashed in picture frames in her mind. She could see nothing of the world—only with her mind's eye, as her eyes no longer existed. She was weightless. She felt like she was still alive, still a conscious being, but she was not. As the sound of wind subsided and the brightness faded, she found herself in dark space. All was silent. A small beam of light broke through the darkness. She tried to lift a pair of hands that no longer existed. Nothing, no one did. Only her crippled and broken awareness. She was composed merely of her unphysical mind. She felt transparent, but she wasn't, because there was nothing left of her.

Her consciousness was back in the nursery, and it detected a dark spirit standing next to her daughter's crib. Next to the crib was a pile of ash.

Zilda looked up, exposing her perfect teeth and smile. Her long glossy platinum waves danced from side to side as she swished her body, searching with her bright eyes for the last sparks of Julia's soul.

Julia's everything turned to nothing.

BREAKAWAY

ANGELA
Fall
Early 1970s

Ed rocked back and forth before he said anything. "I'm sorry dear, ya real motha' made me do the scary things. It was for ya, though. I was ta watch over ya, that's it. To protect ya. And I promised her, that stubborn lil' mother of yours, that I would. I didn' wanna ya to hurt from knowin' the truth." His voice shook. "You shouldn' know 'bout what we've been through on the streets. We was different people back then. She helped me become Edward Bile, and I promised to help her."

Angela threw her hands up in the air. "Get out. Both of you just get out. I need to be alone." She shoved Liam and Ed out of the front door and locked it. She sat by the door. An hour must have passed, but she didn't notice the time. The doorbell rang again.

"I told you to leave me alone," she snapped as she swung the door open.

Caiden stood on the other side of the door. Eyebrows pinched together in concern. "I, um, I was worried about you," he said. He held flowers in hand.

Her heart skipped. "Caiden." An earthy scent swirled in the air around him. She wanted him next to her. But she was such a mess.

"Can I come in?" he asked.

"No. Please I need to be alone."

"What is going on? Is something wrong?" he asked. He stood, respectfully observing her, and this made Angela's heart ache all the more. He was kind and sweet.

As much as she wanted to let him in, to let him hold her, to let him tell her everything would be ok, she was not ready to deal with the situation between them. "Please, just go. Please go." She slammed the door in his face and ran upstairs to pack.

She decided she would put the story on Jack Roe together and go down to the station to report it. As soon as that was done, she would leave New York behind, maybe just for a little while.

◈

The next morning, Angela phoned Liam.

"I'm sorry about last night, I was a mess. I wanted to tell you that the breakthrough story on Jack Roe will be ready this week. I have some loose ends to tie up with the police, FBI, and forensics. I'll be leaving once I'm done with my report. I'm going to take a trip to Italy to get myself together. I will write you. And I will miss you."

"Don't go. I'm here for you. And Caiden's going mad with concern. What happened last night?"

"Liam, please don't start. Please don't ask me to stay or mention Caiden."

"Fine. I understand that you need to be alone," he said. But she could still hear that tone in his voice. He wasn't good at hiding his anger and disappointment.

"Did you speak to your mom about last night?"

"Yes. Apparently, she knew that my father had another woman. But she had no idea about you or the reason why he left us as he did."

"What did you tell her?"

"I couldn't give her a reason. I think she made peace with it a long time ago. The fact that now she knows he didn't just up and abandon us made it a bit easier on her, I guess. It's closure." Liam sighed and continued. "She also said that you are part of the family, and she will never deny it. She wants to talk to you."

Angela gripped the phone tighter and shook her head. "No, I'm not ready."

Liam sighed. "Well, whenever you *are* ready, please come home."

A NEW CHAPTER

Angela secluded herself in a studio apartment next to the Garden of Ninfa in Italy. A quiet place, away from civilization.

The Ninfa's oasis gardens, and the river dividing them were exactly what Angela needed to spark her imagination when writing. She worked day and night writing about investigative journalism. Once she was done with one book, she moved on to others. She mainly wrote to get away from her thoughts. After all, in her imaginary worlds, she could be anybody she wanted to be.

It had been two years, and she was able to put everything that happened out of her mind, but one thing always crept in. Caiden. At times she wanted to quit this silly idea of secluding herself in Italy and go back to New York, knock on his door, and kiss him. Regardless of their relationship. She felt a bit guilty. She wondered if he still felt the same about her. There were so many hurdles. Time had passed. Angela knew well that the world could change in a week. How much Caiden's world had changed since she'd left, she didn't know. Certainly, he would not want to date her if they were related? She wanted to stop thinking about him, but she couldn't.

Angela finished up her fifth novel after another year had passed. At that point, she felt rested and as healed as she would ever be. She decided to return to New York.

Her first stop was the mansion. She unpacked her bags and went down to the kitchen. She didn't think twice before she sat down next to the phone and dialed Liam's number.

"Hey Liam."

"Angela!" he exclaimed. "Where have you been? It's been ages. I hate you for leaving like this and not keeping in touch. You said you would write me. I never got a letter."

"I know. I am so sorry. I should have kept that promise, but I desperately needed time to learn who I was, you know? I had no idea. My entire life I was someone else, something for someone. I only felt like myself when I pursued investigating and writing. I just... I needed to be alone to figure all that out."

"Ok, Angela," Liam replied in a sympathetic tone. "That makes sense. I get that. Did you figure it all out?"

Angela smiled. "I don't know, but I sure tried. Anyway, listen, I'm back in New York. I want to see you."

"Oh that's... that's great because we're actually all getting together at my mom's tonight. Would You come with me? I'm going to be there in an hour or so." The tone of his voice unsettled her.

"Is there something else you want to tell me?" she asked.

"Well, just come to my mom's. Don't worry, ok?"

Angela wanted to use her mind-reading abilities. But she pushed that thought out of her mind.

"Doesn't sound great Liam. What's going on?" She wondered whether she even wanted to go there after everything had been out in the open.

If she did, she would see Caiden. And he was the main reason she had wanted to return so badly.

"Let's just meet there," she said, waiting for Liam's confirmation. She heard a dial tone. How dare Liam leave her on her toes like that? She sighed. She hadn't even unpacked her suitcases. Still exhausted from her trip, she tried to ground herself back at home. She decided to tell Caiden how she felt. And why she left. That they were probably related. And take him up on that first date, assuming he, for whatever reason, would agree to it. She'd at least apologize for shutting him out that horrible night years ago.

Angela put on a pair of jeans and a white blouse. She combed her hair and gathered it into a ponytail. She adorned her lips with a clear gloss then looked in the mirror. Not bad for a jet-lagged Angela. She didn't need much makeup anyway. She left for Liam's mother's house.

❦

Lisa answered the door, and as soon as she saw Angela, she gave her an enormous hug. A tear traveled down her cheek.

"Welcome, dear. I'm so happy you decided to come. I hope you know that you are part of this family, and you will always be treated like family." She wiped the tears away and said, "I want to chat with you. I have so many questions. But not tonight. Come in, the whole family is in the backyard celebrating."

They walked to the backyard. The whole family was present, as well as a few people Angela did not know. The guests smiled, laughed, and casually sipped out of champagne glasses. She eagerly searched for Caiden. She ran over unfamiliar faces at the bar and by the pool before she spotted him sitting on one of the tables and chatting with people she didn't know. As she looked his way, it was as though he felt her presence and he turned to meet her eyes.

How stupid she had been to shut him out. She was angry with herself for not giving him a chance. She saw it now. He was hers, and she was his. But things were different, and if Liam was right that he was from another father or maybe adopted, she was ready to explore what could have happened those four long years ago, between them. They locked eyes, but Liam interrupted the moment.

He ran toward her, screaming. "Angela! I missed you!" He gave her one of the biggest smiles she'd ever seen. She couldn't help but return it. Layla followed Liam, and while holding a toddler in one hand, she gave Angela a quick hug with the other.

"Congratulations Layla," Angela said with a warm smile, tickling the baby's cheek.

"Thank you. His name is Tyler, *and* he is twelve months old today," Layla proudly announced.

"Oh. We're celebrating Tyler's birthday! I wish I'd known. I would have brought gifts!" Angela exclaimed.

"Well, it's not just a celebration for him. It's a joint celebration, sorta. And don't worry about gifts. We have everything we need. Today we are celebrating—" Before Layla could finish her sentence, Angela heard Caiden's voice behind her.

"Angela."

Her temperature must have gone up three-fold when she saw how his warm gaze hugged her. His luscious mouth made her body tremble. Why did she feel this way around him?

"Hi," she shyly said and added, "I need to speak with you. Um, privately if we could. And as soon as possible. Can we..." she stopped. Something in his eyes was different. A little chill. Among the warm haze of longing, there was a coldness. He'd also broken their secret comforting eye lock.

She followed his gaze, which trailed off to a brunette, wearing an off-white strapless dress that extended a little below her knees. Sparkling crystals were sewn into the delicate fabric and seemed to light up her green eyes.

She approached them, flipping her long brown hair from her shoulders. The way she walked toward them reminded Angela of a cat ready to attack its prey. Slow, cautious, but confident. Something about her reminded Angela of a snake. When stood face to face with Angela, her bulging green eyes bubbled with greed and wariness. Her pale thin lips were a bowtie of arrogance.

"May I be introduced?" she smacked her toothpick lips in a heavy English accent. Right away Angela noticed how the woman laced her fingers into Caden's. Locking them in, looking at Angela as if she were a dirty duster.

"So sorry," Caiden cleared his throat. "Ahem. Drina, please meet Angela. Angela Wise, family, and friend all in one. Angela, this is Drina, my fiancée."

Angela felt the color leave her face. She had to balance herself on Liam's shoulder, a common prop for steadiness. Her heart was lost somewhere. She closed and opened her mouth. Her first attempt to speak failed. She managed a smile. "Very nice to meet you. And congratulations to both of you."

Drina looked Angela up and down again, mumbling something under her breath. Lacing her arms around Caiden's neck the way she did made her look like clingwrap.

"Darling. This party is a bore." She continued to hang on to his neck. "My friend just came in. I want to introduce you. Come on." She pulled Caiden after her. Holding on to his arm, constricting like a snake.

"Well," Angela said to herself, looking down to the ground.

"Angela, I wanted to tell you, but I couldn't, and you were going to find out anyway. Better now than later. Better like this."

"Thank you, Liam, for being a jerk." Angela didn't want to hear Liam's apologies. How could he bring her here just to see for herself? He couldn't have told her over the telephone? She was left speechless and lost in her thoughts. *It's been three years, and Caiden has moved on. Obviously, he moved on. Why would he wait for me? He didn't even know if I was coming back. He barely knew me, and I disappeared.* She tried to calm herself until Layla interrupted her thoughts.

"As I wanted to say before I was interrupted," Layla's blue eyes got wider, "we are actually celebrating Caiden's engagement."

"How festive," Angela managed.

Liam took her hand and dragged her inside the house. "I need to talk to you."

"Don't. You've done enough."

"Please. I know what you think. But I brought you because I care about you. You're not here because I'm an inconsiderate asshole."

"Really? You aren't one? Then why?"

"I wanted you to come here—that way, Caiden could see you, and... I don't know, maybe think about leaving that horrible woman."

"You know? I gotta do a story on you, Liam. The inconsiderate jerk who made his best friend suffer, part two."

"Yeah, I'm sorry you had to find out this way. But I see how you guys look at each other, and you are so much better for him than she is. You'd be great together. And I also know he cares about you as much as you care about him."

"So, what am I supposed to do? March over there and steal him? He is engaged for crying out loud. And holy shit, have we forgotten the major problem?" Angela wanted to smack herself. She shouldn't have been angry with Liam. At all. Last he knew, she didn't want to be with Caiden. At least, that was the last thing she'd told him about the situation.

"He does not love her. That worm. She's a smart one. I have no idea how she wrapped him around her finger like that." Liam seemed to be deep in thought. "I know Caiden. He would never go for someone like her."

"I have to go. Goodbye." Angela turned away and took a few steps before Liam grabbed her arm.

"No. Please help me get rid of her. You belong with him."

"I can't deal with your wild suggestions, Liam. There is no way I'm going to break them up. And this is probably for the best, you know, considering... Oh my God, I've lost my mind. I'm sorry. I'm going home. I hope your brother, er, our... I hope Caiden finds someone special, I do. Maybe Drina isn't so bad, you know?" She leaned in close so that only Liam could hear her. "At least she's not possibly his sister."

Liam sighed. "Angela, wait, I don't—" But she took off before he could utter another syllable.

෪

With a tall glass of red wine in her hand, Angela stared into space thinking about how she missed the chance of getting to know the man of her dreams, and she only blamed herself for it. There was nothing she could do now. She had work to do, and she hoped that would take her mind off things.

The trilling of the phone made her jump, and she slowly walked to pick up the receiver.

"Hello?"

"Angela. Please don't hang up," Caiden urgently blurted out on the other line. "I desperately, absolutely, need to speak with you. Please."

"Ok, so speak."

"In person, I need to see you. I'm coming over right now. I should be there in about thirty minutes."

"No. Wait. What?" But all she heard in response was a dial tone.

Angela picked up her glass of wine and took a few sips. She felt a hint of excitement. Butterflies fluttered in her stomach. She hated herself for wanting to see him. It was pointless. Pointless because he was engaged to someone else. Pointless because he was her half-brother. She told herself. If they were blood-related... then, no... just no. No reason to think of what-ifs. She also hated Liam for putting the thought in her head that Caiden still wanted her.

She was a mess when she looked in the mirror. She still cared how she looked enough to pull her hair back in a high ponytail and wash her face. Her eyes were still puffy from all the crying she'd done since she arrived home. She dabbed them with cold water, which seemed to help a little.

Three soft knocks. She'd never felt her heart hammer like that as she made her way to the door.

"May I come in?"

She looked down at the floor because she knew if she locked eyes with him, she would grow weak, and he would see it. She led him inside. Caiden followed her into the living room. She needed to do something, anything, just so she wouldn't look into his eyes. She picked up her wine glass and drank its contents.

Caiden broke the silence. "I'm so happy you're back."

"Are you?" Angela asked, not hiding the sharpness in her voice.

They had only seen each other several times. Why was she behaving this way?

"I have been looking all over for you. I've been to Italy, but you were impossible to find. I've searched for you and always came back disappointed. I couldn't work. Or eat, or sleep. I don't know what it is between us, but I know I want to be with you."

"How convenient. Let's get hitched," she mocked him.

"Angela" he moved in a little closer, and she could see the different colors playing in his eyes. The icicles had melted.

"You are engaged. I'm not enough of a fool to fall for this." She threw her hands up in the air. "Whatever this is."

"I had to get my mind off of you. I knew that if I didn't move on, I would never be able to lead a normal life."

"That's wrong on so many levels Caiden. And we just... can't."

"Nothing you say will make me stop wanting you. What was I supposed to do?"

"What am *I* supposed to do? Accept the fact that you can just marry someone on a whim, to forget about me? What kind of person does that?"

"A person who can't get you out of his head. Angela, we just started to get to know each other. I knew that if we continued, you would be mine forever, and that is what I wanted. It's been three hard years. You just disappeared." Caiden took a deep breath and continued, "You didn't say where you went, or if you would ever come back. I've asked Liam to give you messages from me, but he didn't know where to find you either. We both went to Italy on two different occasions."

Angela was surprised and touched that Liam had taken him all the way to Italy not once, but twice while she was absent, and felt a brief flash of guilt before returning to the subject at hand. "I can't, Caiden. I cannot be the cause of your break-up with your fiancée. This is just too much."

He moved in even closer and placed his arm around her shoulder. Angela trembled, she wanted him even closer, and she wanted more. But she couldn't allow it, not when he was engaged, not when there was a possibility they were related.

"Don't," she commanded him. She wished she could block out her feelings for him, by using one of her spells. But if she did, would the ground open up again? Would she see herself in the dark place below the earth? Would she reawaken something bigger than she imagined possible?

"Angela please don't push me away. We've been through a lot together, and I know it was a while ago, but something like that... it keeps you connected with a person."

"I don't want anything to do with you. Not while you are engaged to another woman."

It seemed Caiden did not hear a word Angela was saying "All I want to do is hold you and make you mine." He inched in closer, she imagined the sweet taste of his lips on hers. He lifted her face to his and brushed his lips against hers.

The warm sensation of his lips sent a shock through her body. She trembled, giving in to his embrace. She was wishing for more than the delicious kiss. As he explored her mouth with his tongue, she pulled away, breathing heavily. She tried to stand up to get away from him, but her legs betrayed her.

❧

Outside the mansion, through the large living room windows, Drina watched all the happenings of the night. Drina, obsessed more with Caiden's money than with him, was slyly spying on them.

When she saw Angela back at the party, the way she looked at him, she knew that woman was trouble. Angela was everything Drina was not. A sweet innocent girl, with kind features, and stunning yet simple beauty.

The worst thing wasn't how the woman looked at Caiden. She could have brushed that off, had she not seen the way Caiden had looked at Angela. Her blood had boiled. When Caiden drove Drina home after the party, she decided to follow him. As she watched the two love birds cuddling on the couch, she picked on the green bush by the window and tore out its leaves. She wanted to scratch her eyes out and watch the blood gush from the blind holes she left behind. She wanted her dead. Caiden never looked at her the way he looked at Angela. Now that she saw their kiss, she wanted to break down the window and drag Angela out of there by her bushy red curls.

❧

Caiden casually ignored her when Angela pulled back. He dove in for another kiss, a wave of warmth and love enclosed her as soon as his lips touched hers. The push to keep going was so strong. But the pull to stop everything had its own strength. She backed away again, this time she was successful. "Stop."

Caiden pulled back. "No? Not good?" he said half-joking, half-concerned.

"No. I mean yes." She shook her head. "No. It's not good. You're engaged. We barely know each other. And... we can't do this, at least not yet. I can't let you hurt that woman. I can't let myself get into this mess. You promised to marry her, probably asked her even. This is wrong in many, many ways. You have to leave. Now."

Angela got up to stand next to the fireplace, as far from him as possible. She pointed to the door. This was so hard for her. She wanted to scream at him to stay and kiss her more, longer.

Caiden tried to protest.

Angela wasn't having it. "I need you to go. And you need to sort things out with Drina. I need time before anything like this happens again." *I need time to know if we are half brother and sister*, she wanted to tell him. But what if they weren't? This thought gave her hope, but there were so many variables. What if that was true? They weren't related, and Caiden didn't know that Jack Roe wasn't his father. Did she want to ruin that for him?

This time, Caiden respectfully obeyed, just before going to the driveway, he said, "Just so you know, I will drive down there right now and break it off with Drina. I was stupid not to do that first. I'm sorry. I'm not some weasel. I don't cheat... I mean, I didn't. I wouldn't. Before. Or again. I'm determined to see how things go between us. I mean... my feelings for you are so much stronger than they are for Drina, even though yeah, maybe I don't know you as well as I should. By all means, I have no right to feel this way. You do too, though. I can tell. I can feel that. I don't want to start off like this, either. Ok? If I do that, would you please give me a chance?"

Angela took a deep breath. She was relieved and horrified. She didn't want to repeat the mistakes her mother had made. She didn't want to break up a relationship and have that tear at her until she turned to dust. But she knew that if she let him stay, they would end up waking up together the next morning. She didn't want that. Not before she was brave enough to tell him the truth. To get clarity. She was proud of herself for being strong enough to show him out. She could now go to bed and reimagine the kiss a million times in her dreams.

As she collected her wine glass from the living room to take it to the kitchen, she heard the doorbell ring.

"You don't give up, do you?" she said as she opened the door. But instead of Caiden's warm dark eyes, a pair of venomous green eyes stared back at her.

Angela couldn't hide her surprise. "Drina?"

Drina pushed Angela out of the way to welcome herself into the mansion. She looked around admirably, then focused on Angela.

"Drina, what are you doing here?"

 "Oh, I don't think I owe you anything. Why don't *you* explain what my fiancé was doing here?"

Angela tried to play innocent, something that had often worked on men. "What are you talking about?" she asked. Seeing Drina's face, Angela knew her act had no effect.

"Oh, don't play stupid. I saw you two. Locking lips, I saw the way he looks at you. How dare you. You slut." Drina snapped, landing her heavy palm across Angela's face.

It was only then, with the woman right in front of her, that Angela realized how much taller Drina was, and she felt as if she would be crushed to the bone. But she managed a harsh reply.

"Look, maybe I deserved that. But you have no right spying on me, forcing your way into my home, or threatening me."

"I have every right, as you felt that you had the right to steal my fiancé."

"I did no such thing."

"Then explain to me what in the world I saw? When you couldn't keep your tongue in your mouth." Drina was cornering Angela, not letting her guard down.

"Maybe you're asking the wrong person. Your fiancé should explain, not me. Now get out of my house," Angela screamed.

"And he will tell me that he loves you and he's leaving me, right?"

"I don't know what he will tell you."

"All this time, I was fighting to get Caiden and I did, and then you came along. With your perfect smile and your perfect everything. Just so you know, you will not be the cause of our breakup." Drina got so close to Angela's face that Angela could smell the alcohol on her breath.

"He is mine, and he will always be mine, and if I must get rid of you to make that happen, I will." Drina put her large hands around Angela's neck and squeezed. Angela struggled for air.

But she felt the grip tighten until her head felt fuzzy, light. She tried to kick, flailed her arms and legs but she couldn't escape. Drina was surprisingly strong.

Angela's eyes closed, and the room went from blurry to white, back to blurry again. She heard Drina repeat; "You will not be the cause of our breakup, no one will stand in my way, no one."

Angela had little choice, either she was going to die or do the one thing she promised Zilda she never would. She didn't have time to think about her options. She remembered Zilda's warning not to use magic. Again, the words in her mother's letter came back to her: *...you must be sure to never practice magic yourself. For if you will it will ignite the evil to reawaken.* She used whatever strength she had left within her and concentrated as she repeated a release spell over and over in her mind. Within seconds, she felt relief in her neck, and she was able to open her eyes. She gasped for air as she looked around.

Where did Drina go? What did I do to her? She hadn't used magic in years. She wasn't even sure if she did it right. The little magic she used in the past by mistake, prompted the ground to open up.

She felt something slimy wriggling at her feet, and when she looked down, she saw a green garter snake trying to wrap itself around her legs. Because it wasn't big, and the snake's attempt to envelop Angela's leg failed.

Angela quickly pulled a coat from the closet beside the entrance door. She threw it over the snake. She ran to the kitchen and grabbed a large jar to contain the reptile. She took a closer look inside the container once she had it captured. She was horrified when she saw its little face up close. The snake had Drina's venomous green, human eyes.

Angela felt a sense of panic. She had no idea how to turn Drina back, nor had she had any intention of turning her into a snake in the first place. She carefully placed the container on the floor. Her head was spinning. She was lightheaded and shaken up, probably from summoning such a large spell after nearly being choked to death.

"To turn someone takes the energy from all four corners of the world. Very few had the power to turn. It's not safe for the body and one might faint within minutes." That's what Zilda told her years ago when they were learning shift spells.

She barely made it to the living room couch. Within moments, she was deeply asleep.

She was awakened by a trembling. Before she opened her eyes, she thought the shaking was internal, but once she was fully conscious, she could see it in the air. The room was cold.

She saw a figure. Humanoid, but much larger. It had extra-long legs, which appeared to have hooves. The figure had six fingers lit up with fire on both its hands and feet, four pointy ears, two on each side, a nose covering almost the whole face lengthwise, and a tail wavered back and forth. The creature had a third eye above the bridge of his nose.

This startled her. She sat up, chilled sweat drenching her face and her pulse racing. What an odd dream. But not all of it had been. She remembered the container, Caiden, and Drina, who was now in a jar in her home.

Angela's light-headed state lifted. She was able to get up and walk over to the container. Drina slithered from side to side, her eyes full of human fury.

"I'm sorry, Drina. I had no idea that I would turn you into this creature." She put on her scarf with one hand while holding the container with the other and jumped in the car.

"I can't let anyone see you. I can't let you stay with me. But you will be safe by the river. I'll visit you. We'll find ways to communicate. And I promise I will figure out a way to turn you back."

Drina's tail violently whipped against the glass. Her eyes told Angela that she was scared.

"I will try and find a way to fix everything."

Angela saw a large, human-sized tear drop from the snake's left eye.

And felt hers dampen, too. She had not liked Drina. But she also never wanted to bring her harm. *How horrified she must be.* Angela was determined to find a way to help the woman.

THE HAPPY DAYS

The days were getting colder and shorter. Angela worried about Drina. She visited her at least once a week. She told her what was going on in the world, kept her company. Even brought her food. But Drina couldn't eat most of it. Most of the time the snake's eyes were filled with sadness. Angela couldn't stop thinking about her or trying to bring her back, but her magic was always misdirected. She'd change other creatures, grow dizzy, fall asleep, see that same demon-like thing. But she'd tried, and it hurt so much that even when Caiden came over, Angela had a frown.

She hadn't seen him in a few days, and she wanted to keep it that way for now. But of course, Caiden phoned and the next thing she knew, he was at her doorstep.

"It is the weirdest thing. I couldn't find her anywhere, and then I got this." Caiden handed Angela a letter.

"To Caiden from Drina," Angela read until Caiden spoke.

"Did you finish reading it? The part where she said she left back to England."

"Yes," Angela replied, lips curved down to her chin. She stood up from the kitchen stool She needed him to follow her, get him closer to the front door.

"Well? You see. She never loved me. She said it herself in the letter. And I never loved her. I went straight to break things off with her, but she was just gone. Then I find this," he said. He jumped up to follow her into the hallway.

The letter I wrote, Angela wanted to say but held back. At least she told Drina she had done it. At which Drina slid away to hide in a pile of dry leaves.

"So, I guess everything's officially over between Drina and me. You know, I was kind of mad that she was only after my money, but I'd lied to her, too. I never loved her. Hell, I cheated on her." He sighed. "I was a jerk. I'm so sorry. I... has enough time passed? I still want... I still... why does this have to be so complicated?" He placed both hands behind his head and paced before settling down a bit. "Look, let me start over. How about that first date?" Caiden offered.

"No. I can't. And please don't ask me again."

"What? Why? I would understand if it's because you didn't trust me. But I swear, I would never act that way again. I'm not a cheater. Will you at least think about it?" he leaned in closer.

Angela shook her head. "I just can't. Not until I find out what I need to find out. Not until I'm ready to find out. Let's leave it at that."

"Find out what? You know what, Angela? No. I don't want to just leave it at that. I don't know what you're afraid of, or what you're hiding from. Because obviously, you're into me as much as I'm into you."

"Please don't question my reasons."

"I know how you feel about me, I see it in your eyes, and definitely felt it in that kiss a few weeks ago." He took a step closer to her. He seemed terrified, but he still did it. He was going for it.

Angela took a step back, she knew that if he came any closer, she would find herself deep in his arms, locking her lips with his.

"It's no use, Angela. You can try and hide your feelings, but I see through it." He took her hand and pulled her close, pressing his lips against hers. Her mouth opened in response, and she found herself in a whirlpool of ecstasy. He pressed his lips harder to hers as she involuntarily caressed his neck. His mouth traveled to her collarbone as he planted gentle kisses on it that sent shivers down her spine. Drinking in his scent with her eyes closed, she enjoyed his dominance.

"You can't begin to imagine what you do to me," he whispered.

If only *he* knew what he did to her. Her insides burned with desire as she felt him lift his hands off her waist to cup her breasts, he lifted her blouse to kiss around her nipples. Angela moaned. She was giving in to him. He had his mouth on her breasts and his hands on her waist. She was too weak, and he knew exactly how to melt her. She wanted to feel his lips on hers once again, she lifted his chin, opening her mouth in anticipation of feeling his lips on hers once again. He pulled away, not allowing her that pleasure.

He had her right where he wanted her, hot for him and desperate.

"So, what do you say about that first date Angela?" he asked, voice steady. Staring at her half-naked breasts, satisfaction gleaming in his deep brown eyes.

How could he? Leave her vulnerable like that? Blushing, she tried to tuck her blouse in, but her shaking hands didn't allow her that small feat.

She knew it was pointless arguing with him. "One date. Just one and that's it." *And that's after I speak with Liam*, she thought.

"Why Angela, why? What we have is obvious. It's real... so, why won't you give us a chance for something bigger?"

"Because I can't, Caiden." How was she supposed to tell him that she decided not to have children? After what she knew about what had happened to her mother. What had happened to Zilda. If she had a child, she was likely only going to continue that cycle. But that was thinking too far ahead.

"You have to do better than that, Angela."

"I don't want to talk about it. Either accept that date or leave."

She knew she was frustrating him, especially after all the effort he'd just put in. Deep down, she felt a wave of satisfaction for getting him angry as she played hard-to-get.

He took a step closer to her, in a split second, he ripped her blouse off her body. He grabbed her breasts viciously and placed his mouth on them again. She couldn't help but allow him to have his way with her.

He unzipped her skirt and threw it to the floor, traveling down, he explored her center with his fingers as she moaned with need. His erection toughened against her bare thigh. As he pressed further into her, he abruptly stopped.

"You... you haven't done this before." He caught his breath and lowered his hand.

She blushed. She saw him take deep breaths, trying to cool himself off. He picked up her blouse and handed it to her. She took offense, not knowing if he was just trying to distract himself from her. He left and returned with two glasses of cool water.

"Here drink something," he said. She took the glass, her hands still shaking from the sweet adrenaline her body endured a few minutes ago.

She was about to give herself to him all the way. She hated herself. The power he had over her seemed surreal. She took a few deep breaths and a gulp of water. He deserved to know the truth. At least part of it.

"Thank you for stopping. And you're right, what we have is rare, and the reason I don't want to get involved is that I know how much you adore children. And I know we are not there, but if you talk about us being together or trying... regardless of whether things work out or if we do try. You should know that I can't have them... children." And she also wanted to tell him, to ask him if he had another father. But did she want to hurt him. What if he didn't know? What if she would ruin his life by telling him, by asking him?

He was silent. Staring at his glass.

Was he upset? Had he changed his mind about her?

He cupped her face in his hands. "I care about you, Angela. Like really care about you a whole lot. I do love children, and if our relationship goes where I want it to... we'll figure something out, ok? It doesn't matter to me. At all. This doesn't mean there won't be children in the future. And you know what? If there aren't, maybe that's just the way things will be, and things will be fine."

Angela smiled. For the first time since her accident, she felt almost weightless. While she still didn't know the full truth, his kindness was unbearably heartwarming. He was such a good guy. She wrapped her arms around his neck and showered him with a million kisses.

A FRESH START

The morning sun peeked through the window, as the birds sang their morning summer songs. Her heart raced with anticipation, her stomach flipped and flopped. Today was a day Angela thought would never come.

She twirled her engagement ring. Her mind was stuck on the imagery of her walking down the aisle to meet her husband-to-be. She was surprised she was even able to sleep at all the past few days.

Angela and Caiden wanted a simple small wedding, so they decided to do the ceremony in a casual hall on Long Island. They had invited only close family and Ed. She visited Drina by the lake just a few days prior. She decided not to add to the snake's misery and skipped telling her about the wedding. The snake moved smoothly over Angela's left hand and situated herself on it. Angela forgot to remove her engagement ring. Surprisingly, Drina didn't look angry. Instead, her eyes pleaded with Angela. "I'll find a way out for you, Drina, I promise. And I know I keep saying that. But I mean it."

It was mid-morning, Liam was waiting downstairs, as Angela donned her charmeuse sheath dress with a lace halter.

"You look stunning as usual, but today you are something else," Liam said with a huge smile, after she opened her door to him.

"Thank you, brother."

"Are you ready?"

"Yes."

A white daisy with a yellow stigma was pinned to her hair, Liam adjusted her veil. "Let's go then."

"Thank you for pushing me to get to know him."

After her first date with Caiden, Angela felt that she was already in too deep to tell him the whole truth. She feared asking about his past, about his family; she feared that he would easily figure her out; he'd understand that, because Angela knew she Liam's sister, she also thought she and Caiden might be related. She had put off telling him the truth for so long that this was now her own quiet, personal secret.

But she had still needed to know. For herself. So, she put her journalism skills to work and did some digging.

Much to her relief, she discovered that Caiden had been adopted by the Roe family when they found out they couldn't have more children.

This was wonderful and this was terrible, because the worst part of it all was that she had agreed to marry him before she knew herself. The two had shared moments of intimacy while she was uncertain. She was angry with herself over this simple fact because again, she couldn't help but feel that she was repeating the mistakes of the generations of women who had come before her. Lying, hiding. She wanted, instead, to learn from those mistakes. Perhaps one day, she would be able to tell him the truth.

All of Angela's guilt faded when they reached the hall. Liam walked her down the aisle. Caiden was beaming. The officiant was quick and effective. The two sealed their union with a sweet kiss.

After the ceremony, Caiden carried his bride in his arms into their new home in the city. He asked her to close her eyes carrying her into their bedroom. The bed was decorated with a thousand multicolored rose petals.

This was the happiest day of her life. She forgot about her horrible past, and Delirium, and the promise of a cursed world. She forgot about everything other than the happiness she felt with her husband.

She returned his kisses, as he caressed every inch of her body. Untying the back of her dress, he kissed her shoulders, his mouth traveled down to her breasts where he stopped for a moment to tease her.

"Finally. I get to have you," he said, his voice hoarse.

He lifted his mouth to her lips, and she tasted herself on him. He teased her with his fingers. She motioned him to lift to her mouth. She found him looking into her dazzling eyes, taking in her sweet smell, lowering his body, he positioned himself matching her. Until they both found pleasure in each other.

❦

They entered, together, a new era. The 1980s. Everything was sort of wonderful. After a life of feeling as though she'd been used by others, abandoned, and tossed aside, being married to Caiden felt like heaven. Things settled down. Drina was still miserable in her snake form, and Angela was still trying to figure out how to fix her without summoning that horrid figure again. But now was not the time to think about all that.

Now she had to figure out why she had been feeling so ill. She was sitting comfortably in the doctor's office. Leaning back while waiting for her blood results. She flipped through a magazine, picking out a new rug for the bedroom. The doctor said it might be a hernia since the sonogram ruled out pregnancy. That was exceptionally good news. She was on the pill. So, they didn't know why she was feeling nauseous and weak, and at the same time always hungry. She'd taken around a dozen blood tests to figure it out.

"Mrs. Roe." The Dr. stretched out his hand "Got your blood results ready here."

"Will I live?" she joked

"Yep. Congratulations. Bloodwork confirmed pregnancy."

Her face turned hot, and her heart skipped a few beats. She wasn't sure if it was from excitement or fear.

"But how? It can't be. The sonogram?"

"Sometimes the baby hides, and we can't always pick up the heartbeat when a woman is early in pregnancy."

Chills ran down her spine. "But... no. No, that can't be right."

"I assure you that it is," the doctor said.

Angela began to tear up. "No. No. I was so careful. I took the pills from day one."

"Well, the pill is not a guarantee, Mrs. Roe."

"How far along am I?"

"One month."

Angela put her hands over her flat belly, involuntarily caressing it. Caiden would be thrilled.

But she could not have this child. The world would go to hell if she did.

She panicked. What could she do? Abortion? The thought upset her too much to entertain the notion. No, she didn't have any options. None that she was willing to go through with. Angela was at a loss, and she figured the best she could do was hope for a boy.

As she walked home from the clinic, she kept repeating to herself, *I'm going to be a mother. I'm going to have a child.* And then she felt the cold. She heard the voice.

"I'm thrilled, Angela. Soon, we are coming for you, and for her." It was that demon, that beast. She'd encountered him enough. She believed it was the one that her mother had referred to as Delirium.

"Don't count on it, you beast." Time seemed to stop. Everything froze. Even the leaves stopped moving. Traffic stood still, and people seemed to be painted into the landscape. They were two-dimensional. Motionless. She heard footsteps from behind a tree. She was able to make out his tail behind a thick tree trunk.

"There is nothing you can do now, Ortor. This world will be ours. So many decades of fighting for it. And thanks to you, we will have it at our fingertips."

"I won't rest until I have gotten rid of you forever." Angela tried to sound tough. She tried to make her voice strong and steady. It didn't matter anymore if she used her magic. She had reawakened him; she'd already made the mistake of using her magic when she didn't know how to control it. She had only a second to try to end this now and forever, with magic she never wanted to learn.

You have exceptional powers, Zilda said that to her. Angela believed that she had exceptional powers. She had to try. Her heart pounded as heat rose to her face. Her skin flushed. Everything around her was still, aside from the tail and hooves, which moved so fast. She wondered if she'd done something to him. She envisioned tearing the demon into pieces, grinding him into a fine powder. She moved him from behind the tree, and she was able to see him. He was probably five feet taller than her. She was scared. She tried to stay in control, tried to stay focused, but she felt she was losing strength. As he inched in closer, he opened his mouth. Two rows of sharp teeth and a snake's tongue lashed, slashed the side of her cheek. She saw another movement in his legs. She was doing something, because his tongue retracted back into his giant mouth, and he took a step back. One of his hooves broke off, and with that, she lost her concentration. She heard his unbearable laugh before the ground opened up to swallow him in its core.

Down below the witches gathered by the deep fire lake at the east end. They eagerly waited. Waited to join Delirium at the bloodriver. Their third eyes all glowed a brilliant yellow. Something was happening. They chanted "Dlrm whatm. Dlrm whatm." Rocking their frail bodies from one side to the other looking above, waiting for their time.

The ground opened, filling the stale air below, with something fresh. It gave them a reason to celebrate. They feasted on maggots and spoke of the new world. A world above. A better life, an eternal one.

PREVIEW: BOOK II - DEEP DOWN
BELOW

Angela had to find Briana. She didn't care about the monstrous eyes peeking out of the spiky trees, or the stench of death in the forest, or that she was somewhere underground, beneath the core of the earth, far away from her comfortable home in New York. Far away from Caiden.

She was still surprised that she could breathe or see down here, or that she did not feel the heat of the landscape. She imagined the core of the earth would be hot. She was surprised that she figured out how to reach the underworld. But getting down here was probably normal for someone like her. She was no longer faint of heart. She was a different Angela. She left her old life as a famous reporter, who was comfortably bubbled in her hometown. She forgot the last time she felt mercy, the last time she shared her heart with Caiden. That life... Caiden, all of it was irrelevant. The fact that her daughter was taken by Delirium shaped her up like iron steel, and nothing else mattered.

Angela reached her right arm over to her left shoulder and stroked Drina's silky skin. Drina's head swiveled about, her eyes wide and scanning the landscape before they fell back upon Angela. The two stared at one another.

"I am careful," Angela said to the snake, looking into her bulging eyes. "What would you do in my situation?"

Drina lowered her head and closed her human eyes. Another tear rolled down her face.

The forest was thick with thorn-like trees that branched out in pointy spikes, blocking the view of the sticky path. The thorns were nothing like she'd seen before; they resembled wood and metal at the same time.

Angela had to walk with her fingers pinching her nose to keep out the smell from the plants. They reeked of rotten vegetables and death. She could almost see the green cloud of stench steaming from their thick roots. She also had to keep her hand close to the blade in her left pant pocket.

She heard rustling by the trees to her right. She stopped. The darkness didn't allow her to see much, but a yellow ball-like light shone through. All Angela knew was that whatever it was, it was too close for its own good. The rustling stopped, but the yellow light was still there. Angela's knees hit the slimy bottom. She picked Drina off her shoulder and lowered her to the ground.

"Check it out," Angela whispered, although she felt she didn't have to because the forest was so quiet, Drina probably heard Angela think.

Drina's eyes displayed confidence and bravery. She even looked happy to do something other than sit on Angela's shoulder and cry about the past, and the present.

She slithered away to the right. Within a moment Angela heard Drina his. Then another *Hisssssssss*. Angela felt for the sharp blade in her left pocket. She took it out and passed it to the other hand, gripping onto its handle. Drina was in trouble.

Angela, took a few steps toward the thick trees

"Let her go," she said.

A mild shuffling came from beneath the spiky overgrowth. Angela stood her guard, knife ready in hand. Her feet rooted into the slimy bottom, ready to strike.

Feeling relieved, Angela extended her palms to let Drina crawl back onto her shoulder. Her eyes had a hint of shock in them, like she'd seen something horrific.

"Come out, whoever you are," Angela demanded. She knew running would not help because she had no idea how to navigate these woods.

"No. You come this way," a voice responded. The rasp had notes of femininity in it. Barely detectable.

Angela hesitated. "Who are you? Show yourself first."

"Name is Arcane." A tall figure stepped out of the shadows; a cloak's hood covered most of her face.

Angela felt something squeezing her wrist. She dropped her eyes to her right hand, where she wore the ruby bracelet Liam had given her long ago after his trip to France. The ruby activated. It up and emitted a bright red light. It continued to squeeze Angela's wrist, cutting off circulation. Her whole hand was numb.

"That belongs to me you know," Arcane said, taking another step toward her.